LIN ANDERSON

Driftnet

HODDER

Copyright © 2003 by Lin Anderson

First published in Great Britain in 2003 by Luath Press Ltd

First published in paperback in 2006 by Hodder & Stoughton
A division of Hodder Headline

A Hodder paperback

1

A CIP catalogue record for this title
is available from the British Library

ISBN 0 340 92236 2

Typeset in Plantin by Hewer Text UK Ltd, Edinburgh
Printed and bound by Clays Ltd, St Ives plc

Hodder Headline's policy is to use papers that are natural, renewable
and recyclable products and made from wood grown in sustainable
forests. The logging and manufacturing processes are expected to
conform to the environmental regulations of the country of origin.

Hodder & Stoughton Ltd
A division of Hodder Headline
338 Euston Road
London NW1 3BH

Driftnet

Rhona closed her eyes and tried to relax. She had been at many murder scenes, some more horrible than the one tonight. Death didn't scare her, not when it was reduced to tests and samples. But tonight was different. There was something about that particular boy. Something she hadn't been able to put her finger on. Not until the Sergeant had put it into words for her, coming back into the car.

The boy who had been abused and strangled in that hideous little room looked so like her, he could have been her brother.

About the author

Lin Anderson began writing whilst working as a teacher, and now writes full time. *Driftnet* is her first novel.

Thanks to Emma R. Hart,
BSc, MSc, Forensic Science for her inside knowledge.

To Detective Inspector Bill Mitchell

I

THE BOY DIDN'T expect to die.

When the guy put the tasselled cord round his neck, grinning at him, he thought it was just part of the usual game. The guy was excited, a dribble of saliva slithering down his chin and falling onto the boy's bare shoulder. He nodded his agreement. He was past feeling sick at their antics. He lay back down, turning his head sideways to the greyish pillow that smelt of other games, closed his eyes and shifted his thoughts to something else. There was a goal he liked to play out in his head.

On the right, the Frenchman, arrogant, the ball licking his feet, thrusting forward. The opposition starts to group and there's a scuffle. Bastards. But no worry 'cos the Frenchman's through and running, the ball anchored to him, like a child to its mother. The crowd breathes in. Time stretches like an elastic band. Then the ball's away, curving through the air.

Wham! It's in the net.

The boy can usually go home now. Not this time. This time, before the ball reaches the net, his head is pulled back, then up. The intense pressure bulges his eyes, bursting a myriad of tiny blood vessels to pattern the white. His body spasms as the cord bites deeper, slicing through skin, cutting the blood supply to his brain. At the moment of death his penis erupts, scattering silver strands of semen over the multicoloured cover.

2

SEAN WAS ALREADY asleep beside her. Rhona liked that about him. His baby sleep. His face lying smooth and untroubled against the pillow, his lips opened just enough to let the breath escape in soft noiseless puffs. No one, she thinks, should look that good after a bottle of red wine and three malt whiskies.

Rhona has given up watching Sean drink. It is too irritating, knowing the next morning he won't have a hangover. Instead he'll throw back the duvet (letting a draught enter the warm tent that had enclosed their bodies), slip out of bed and head for the kitchen. From the bed she will watch (a little guiltily), as he moves about; a glimpse of thigh, an arm reaching up, his penis swinging soft and vulnerable. He'll whistle while he makes the coffee and forever in her mind Rhona will match the bitter sweet smell of fresh coffee with the high clear notes of an Irish tune.

They have been together for seven months. The first night Rhona brought Sean home they never reached the bedroom. He held her against the front door, just looking at her. Then he began to unwrap her, piece by piece, peeling her like ripe fruit, his lips not meeting hers but close, so close that her mouth stretched up of its own accord, and her body with it. Then, with a flick of his tongue, he entered her life.

When the phone rang, Sean barely moved. Rhona knew once it rang four times the ansaphone would cut in. The caller would listen to Sean's amiable Irish voice and change their view of answering machines, thinking they might be human after all. Rhona lifted the receiver on the third ring. It would be an emergency or they wouldn't phone so late. When she suggested to the voice on the other end that she would need a taxi, the Sergeant told her that a police car was already on its way. Rhona grabbed last night's clothes from the end of the bed.

Constable William McGonigle had never been at a murder scene before. He had stretched the yellow tape across the tenement entrance like the Sergeant told him and chased away two drunks who thought that police activity constituted a better bit of entertainment than staggering home to hump the wife. Constable McGonigle didn't agree.

'Go home,' he told them. 'There's nothing to see here.'

He was peering up the stairwell, wondering how much longer he would have to stand there freezing his balls off when he heard the sound of high heels clipping the tarmac. A woman leaned over the tape and stared into the dimly lit stair.

'Sorry, Miss. You can't come in here.'

'Where's Detective Inspector Wilson?'

Constable McGonigle was surprised.

'Upstairs, Miss.'

'Good,' she said.

Her fair hair shone white in the darkness and Constable McGonigle could smell her perfume. She lifted a silken leg and straddled his yellow tape.

'I'd better go on up then,' she said.

The click of Rhona's heels echoed round the grimy stairwell, but if she was disturbing any of the residents, they didn't show it by opening their doors. No one here wanted to be seen. If there was a fire they might come out, she thought, in the unlikely event they weren't completely comatose.

A door on the second landing stood ajar. She could hear DI Wilson's voice inside. If Bill was here at least she wouldn't have to explain who she was. She could just get on with the job, go home and crawl back into bed.

The narrow hall was a fetid mix of damp and heat. The sound of her heels died in a dark mottled carpet, curled at the edge like some withered vegetable. She paused. Three doors, all half open. On her right a kitchen, on her left a bathroom. She caught a glimpse of a white suit and heard the whirr of a camera. The Scene of Crime Officers were already at work.

The end door opened fully and Detective Inspector Bill Wilson looked out.

'Bill.'

'Dr MacLeod.'

He nodded. 'It's in here.'

He allowed himself a tight smile. The two other men in the room turned and stared out at her. Dr MacLeod was not what either of them had expected.

Rhona looked down at her black dress and high-heeled sandals. 'I came out in a bit of a hurry.'

'McSween will get you some kit.'

Bill nodded to one of the men, who went out and came back minutes later with a plastic bag.

Rhona pulled out the scene suit and mask, put her coat into the bag and handed it to the officer. She took one shoe off at a time and, hitching up her skirt, slipped her feet into the suit. Only then did she step inside.

Rhona took in the small room at a glance. The hideous nicotine-stained curtains stretched tightly across the window. A wooden chair with a pair of jeans and a tee-shirt thrown over it. Two glasses on a formica table. A pair of trainers on the floor beside the bed. A divan, three-quarters width, no headboard but covered with heavy silken brocade in an expensive burst of swirling colours.

The boy's naked body lay face down across it, his head turned stiffly towards her, eyes bulging, tongue protruding slightly between blue lips. The dark silk cord knotted round the neck looked like a bow tie the wrong way round. The body showed signs of hypostasis, and the combination of dark purple patches and pale translucence reminded Rhona of marble. Below the hips blood soaked into the bedclothes.

'I turned the gas fire off when I arrived,' Bill said. 'The smell nearly finished off our young Constable, so I put him on duty outside for some fresh air.'

'Did anyone take the room temperature?'

'McSween has it.'

Rhona took a deep breath before she put on the mask. The smell of a crime scene was important. It might mean she would look for traces of a substance she would otherwise have missed. Here the nauseating odour of violent death mixed with stale sex and sweat masked something else, something fainter. She got it. An expensive men's cologne.

'McSween and Johnstone have covered the rest of the room. The photographer is working on the kitchen and bathroom.'

'What about a pathologist?'

'Dr Sissons came and certified death. Then suggested I get a decent forensic to take samples and bag the body because he needed to get back to his dinner party.'

'Important guests?'

'He did mention a "Sir" somewhere in the list.'

Rhona smiled. Dr Sissons preferred analysing death in the comfort of his mortuary. Taking samples of bodily fluids in the middle of the night he regarded as her territory.

'That's some bedcover!'

'We think it might be a curtain, but we'll get a better look once we take the body away.'

'Did the doctor turn him over?'

'Just enough to tell if he's been moved. He said the left side of the face, the upper chest and hips had been compressed since death occurred. He's lying where he was killed.'

Rhona opened her case and took out her gloves. She knelt down beside the bed.

'There's a lot of blood under the body.'

Bill nodded grimly. 'You'd better take a look underneath.'

Rhona lifted the right arm and rolled the body a little. The genitals had been gnawed, the penis severed by a jagged gash that ran from the left hand tip to halfway up the right side. One testicle was mashed and hanging by a thin strip of skin.

'This must have been done after he died or the blood would be all over the place.'

'That's what Sissons said.'

Rhona let the body roll back down. The boy's head nestled back into the dirty pillow.

'Any sign of a weapon?'

Bill shook his head. 'Maybe it wasn't a weapon.'

'A biter? Did Dr Sissons check for other bite marks?'

'He muttered something about bruising on the nipples and the shoulder.'

'I'll take some swabs.'

'How long do you think he's been dead?' Bill said.

Rhona pressed one of the deepening purple patches, and watched it slowly blanch under her finger. 'Maybe six, seven hours. Depends on the temperature of the room.'

Bill risked a satisfied smile.

'Matches the Doc.'

Rhona raised her eyebrows a little. She and Dr Sissons didn't usually agree. He had a habit of disagreeing with her on points like the exact time of death.

It was almost a matter of principle. Rhona had done three years' medicine before she switched to forensic science. She liked to practise now and again.

'How did you find him?'

'An anonymous phone call.'

'The murderer?'

'A young male voice. Very frightened. Maybe another rent boy came here to meet a client?'

'Alive, this one would have been pretty,' Rhona said.

Bill nodded. 'Not the usual type for this area,' he said. 'A bit more class, but rented all the same. I'll leave you to it? Just shout if you need anything.'

She was nearly an hour taking samples of everything that might prove useful later on. After she'd finished with the surrounds, she concentrated on the body, under the fingernails, the hair, the mouth. Dr Sissons would take the anal and penile swabs.

The skin felt cold through her gloves, but with the blond hair flopped over the empty eyes, he might have been any teenager fast asleep. Rhona lifted the hair and studied the face, trying to imagine what the boy would have looked like in life. There were none of the tell-tale signs of poor diet and drug abuse. This one had been healthy. So how did he end up here?

'Finished?' Bill's timing was immaculate. 'Mortuary boys are here.' He looked at her face. 'Go home and have a hot toddy,' he said.

A hot toddy was Bill's answer to almost any ailment.

Rhona got up from the bed and unwrapped her hands. 'Any idea who he is?' she said.

'Not yet. But I don't think he was Scottish.' He pointed to the hall. Behind the door hung a leather jacket and a football scarf. 'Manchester United,' he said in mock disgust.

'There are people up here who support Man U,' Rhona suggested cheekily, knowing Bill was a Celtic man.

'Yes, but they wouldn't flaunt it. Not in Glasgow anyway.'

Rhona laughed.

'All right then?'

'Yes.' She began to pack her samples in the case.

'The Sergeant will run you home.'

He walked with her to the front door.

'How's that Irishman of yours these days? Still playing at the club?'

'Yes, he is.'

'Must get down and hear him again soon. Good jazz player. You'll ring me as soon as you've got anything?'

'Of course.'

Sean was still asleep when Rhona got back. With the heavy curtains drawn the room was dark, although outside dawn was already touching the university rooftops. She had stopped at the lab on her way home and checked the swabs for saliva. It was there all right.

She left a note on the bench for Chrissy in case she got there first, giving her a brief history of the night's events, then she headed home for a few hours' sleep.

Rhona pulled her dress over her head, kicked off her shoes and slid under the duvet. She wrapped her chilled body round Sean's. He grunted and moved his arm over to take her hand.

'Okay?' he mumbled.

'Okay,' she said, but he was already back asleep.

Rhona closed her eyes and tried to relax into his warmth. She had been at many murder scenes, some more horrible than the one tonight. Death didn't scare her, not when it was reduced to tests and samples. But tonight was different. There was something about that particular boy. Something she hadn't been able to put her finger on. Not until the Sergeant had put it into words for her, coming back in the car.

The boy who had been abused and strangled in that hideous little room looked so like her, he could have been her brother.

3

WHEN SHE GOT to the lab the next morning, there was a delicious smell of fresh coffee. Someone had been to the Deli, because there were two croissants on a plate next to the machine.

'So you finally decided to come in?' Chrissy's red head appeared round the door of the cupboard. 'Thought I was going to have to do all the work myself.'

'You got my note?'

'I found it,' said Chrissy grimly. 'The samples you brought back are logged, and the bags of clothing and bedclothes arrived about half an hour ago.'

'The croissants look good,' Rhona said, picking one up.

'I thought lover boy made the breakfast,' Chrissy observed tartly.

'I made him stay in bed. It was too early for sane people to be up.'

'You have a man who thinks it's his job to make the breakfast and you stop him doing it.' Chrissy shook her head in disbelief. 'Try getting one of my brothers to do anything in the kitchen.'

'What about Patrick?'

'Patrick was different,' she said flatly. 'That's why he left.'

They sat at the lab table while Chrissy made notes on what was to be done. Rhona had already filled in the background, at least the stuff Chrissy needed to know. She didn't know why she was always so careful of Chrissy's feelings. She might be young but she'd seen plenty in her life, if her tales of her brothers were anything to go by.

Chrissy looked up from her list. 'We're going to be pushed to do all this with Tony away.'

'Unless they draft in some help, we'll just have to put the regular work on hold. Murder has priority,' Rhona said.

'They never gave us any help for the last one.' Chrissy's voice was wearily resigned. 'Have they any idea who the boy was, or do we have to identify him as well?'

'He had no ID on him. We'll profile him on what we have and see what Bill comes up with.'

'I'll start on the clothing then?'

Rhona nodded. 'The cover looks as though it has been used before. I circled areas to be tested.'

'Semen?'

'Probably. Oh, and there was a smell in the room.'

'I bet there was!'

'No. I mean a nice smell. Like a man's cologne. Subtle, probably expensive.'

'Definitely not Brut then?'

'Definitely not your average aftershave. It's a long shot, but maybe there's some on the boy's tee-shirt or that cover.'

'There was plenty of blood.'

'Yes.' Rhona wasn't going to elaborate.

'It's okay. The photos arrived first thing. I've already had a look. Poor guy. Nice looking too.'

She gave Rhona an odd stare. Rhona remembered what the Sergeant had said the night before. But if that was what Chrissy was thinking, she didn't say it.

'That's the problem nowadays, all the nice looking ones are gay.' Chrissy grinned. 'Except your Sean, of course.'

'If you could stop thinking about Sean, we could get started.'

Rhona was trying to pull rank but it was water off a duck's back. Her Scientific Officer gave her a look that said, 'So you didn't get it last night.'

'By the way. There was a phone call for you, Rhona. A bloke. Sounded sexy. Wouldn't give his name. Just said he'd try later.'

Death always involved relationships. Death because they loved you. Death because they didn't. Death because no one loved them. Love and hate. Hate and love.

And what about this death? Why had the boy died? It looked as though he had come to the room for sex. There was no sign of a struggle, not until the noose had tightened round his neck and even then, only when the perpetrator had gone too far.

Dr Sissons had confirmed that death was by asphyxiation during anal sex. The ligature had probably been used to restrict oxygen to the brain to promote orgasm, he said.

'The death wasn't premeditated then?' Rhona asked.

'There's some evidence to suggest the boy has been involved in this sort of activity before. Earlier bruises in the same area, though less pronounced. There was probably a pad placed between the ligature and the neck.'

'But not this time?'

'No. This time, the ligature was tightened to unconsciousness and beyond. Whatever the boy agreed to do, I can't believe he wanted to die.'

'And the mutilation?'

'After death definitely, and probably by biting. The gash on the penis is elliptical. I took the liberty of calling in the Odontology Unit. Hope that's okay?'

Dr Sissons liked to believe there was rivalry between the various forensic departments. Even if there was, Rhona wasn't going to encourage him.

'I located saliva on the nipples and the shoulder,' she said.

'Good. There was also semen on the anal swab. What about the curtain?'

'We're working on that. It looks as though it's been used more than once. We'll take our time and go over all of it. There might be fibres or old blood,' Rhona said. 'Oh, and I combed two head hairs from the pubic region.'

'Not the boy's?'

'I've still to check, but one's dark, so it's unlikely.' Rhona paused. 'I take it you don't know who the boy is yet?'

'No. The post mortem suggests he was in his late

teens, say between sixteen and twenty. Good health. No evidence of drug abuse. Non-smoker. Well nourished. Your forensic biologists are enjoying the dubious pleasure of examining his stomach contents, so we'll know soon what he'd been eating before he died. With a bit of luck it will be curry and the police can start checking all the Glasgow curry houses to see if they recognise him. And Dr MacLeod?' Dr Sissons' voice was thoughtful.

'Yes?'

'You aren't missing a member of your family, are you? The boy bore an uncanny resemblance to you.'

Rhona assured him that as far as she knew, her family was fully accounted for and rang off.

Rhona lifted her head from the microscope. A smirr of rain was touching the window, but here and there the sun was breaking through the cloudy skies. The park below the laboratory was quiet, just a few mums and kids at the swings and a couple walking, arm in arm. As she watched, the boy stopped beside a clump of trees, bent down and picked a bluebell and handed it to the girl. They began to kiss.

Six months before, Rhona had stepped over another yellow tape just where the couple were standing now. It had turned out to be a student, murdered on his way home from a dance at the Students' Union. Last night's murder, she thought, made four in one year. All young men.

The first two had been violent assaults with no evidence of sexual activity, but the one in the park had been different. It had all the hallmarks of queer bashing. The student was gay and was in a known cruising area. His chest and arms were covered with kick marks and his head had been caved in by a blunt instrument, which was never found. The area had been scoured for traces of the killer – or killers. It had been useless. Heavy overnight rain had washed the place clean of clues.

One thing connected that murder to this one. The victim had been wearing a thin leather neck band with a Celtic cross on it. At the post mortem the pathologist had found bruising round the neck, consistent with the neck band being pulled during the assault. What if tightening the neck band had been part of a violent sexual assault?

When Sean found out what her job was, he had laughingly called her Lady Death. Rhona didn't care. She loved her work. She loved the functions and the structures and the painstaking carefulness of it all. She had forsaken medicine because she found it too depressing. So many sick people and, if she was honest, so little she could do to help them. Forensic Science was different. Here she could help, as long as she was prepared to look for the truth. That was the fascination. The truth hid from her, until she found just the right question to ask. At the end of the day, it wasn't what had happened but why it had happened that held the truth.

Maybe that's why we couldn't find the killer, she thought. Maybe we got the 'why' bit of the jigsaw wrong.

The couple had moved off towards the Art Gallery and were climbing the steps to get under the ornate portico, out of the rain. Rhona went back to the microscope, not wanting to think about the Gallery. Not since last Friday when she'd taken her lunch there and spotted the familiar long blue raincoat and dark hair.

She tried to concentrate on the next slide, ignoring the knot in her stomach.

'Fancy coming out for some lunch?' Chrissy was standing in the doorway.

Rhona shook her head.

'Right. I'll bring you back a sandwich then.' Chrissy wasn't asking. She was telling. It was like having your mother working for you.

Rhona watched Chrissy emerge below. A bloke on the other side of the street crossed to meet her, his shaved head bowed and his hands in his pockets. It looked as if Chrissy was giving him a right mouthful. The latest in a long line of boyfriends or one of Chrissy's brothers on the scrounge, Rhona thought.

Bill Wilson contacted her halfway through the afternoon and asked how things were going. She told him what she'd told Dr Sissons.

'I'm working on the hairs just now,' she said. 'It'll take us a while to examine the cover thoroughly, but you can have the whisky glasses back. I've finished with them.'

'Thanks, although I don't hold out much hope of finding our suspect's prints on file.' Bill sounded resigned. 'By the way, the story's splashed all over the evening paper.'

'Right.'

She heard a short 'mmm' of displeasure.

'If anyone pesters you for info?'

'I don't have any. Oh, and Bill.' She hesitated. 'Were you right?' she asked.

'About what?'

'The English connection.'

'We haven't found out who the boy was or where he came from. But you can read that in the *Glasgow News*. They always know more than us anyway.'

Rhona stopped work at five o'clock. Her eyes were tired from peering down the microscope and the lunchtime sandwich had long since been eaten. Chrissy had left at four, pleading a 'domestic' to sort out. One look at Chrissy's face convinced Rhona not to ask any questions.

Now, all she wanted was something substantial to eat and a long hot soak in the bath. But that meant facing Sean. She started to tidy the lab, methodically filing away her notes and storing the samples, putting off the moment when she would have to go home.

Outside, the rain had moved off north towards the Campsie Hills. The sky had cleared to a dull blue. She was a twenty minute walk from the flat and as long as the evening was fine there was no point in taking a bus. It would just sit in traffic anyway. She headed for Byres Road.

She knew Sean would have already bought some-

thing for tea but she stopped at the pasta shop anyway.
Mr Margiotta welcomed her with his usual patter and
persuaded her to try the spinach and ricotta cannelloni,
adding an extra dollop of tomato and basil sauce for
good measure.

'Love food,' he promised with a wicked grin.

Just what she didn't need.

Rhona allowed herself five minutes to decide what she
was going to do, before she put her key in the lock. Part
of her wished she could just forget what she'd seen in
the Art Gallery, but it was like a forensic clue and she
couldn't let it go. Like one of those semen samples. She
had to know whose it was.

When she opened the door of the flat she was
greeted by the rich scents of garlic and olive oil.

'Hi,' Sean called from the kitchen. He was chopping
vegetables next to the cooker. He turned and smiled,
wiping his hands on a tea towel. 'You look tired,' he
said. 'Coffee? A drink?'

'A bath.'

He came towards her and she forced herself to smile.

'Come on,' he said.

She wanted to be in the bathroom alone with the
door locked, but Sean led her in, turned on the taps
and began to undress her. Behind Rhona the water
pounded into the tub, hot and cold, like her thoughts.
He sat on the chair and pulled her onto his knee,
stroking the back of her neck with one hand while
his other tested the water. When it was right, he turned
off the taps.

'Get in. It's fine.' She stepped into the water like an obedient child. 'I'll give you a shout when tea's ready.'

He left the door open when he went out. She leaned over to shut it properly.

'Don't lock it!' he called. 'I'll bring you in a glass of wine.'

Rhona sat down defeated, leaned back and closed her eyes.

Sean came in twice. First with the wine as promised and again with the bottle to refill her glass. Rhona kept her eyes closed the second time, although he knelt beside the bath so that she could feel his warm breath on her face. Then the water parted with her knees, hitting the sides of the bath in a wave of emotion, as he ran his hand slowly up her thigh.

This was what it was like, she thought. To be primed. Made ready. Sean was good at that. She pushed herself up and opened her eyes.

'Okay now?' He was smiling at her, the dark blue eyes full of confidence.

She stood up and he handed her a towel, then the dressing gown.

'Don't bother getting dressed,' he said.

Sean liked women. He was comfortable in their company. But most of all he liked to take them to bed. He played his saxophone with the same sensual concentration he gave to sex. He would cradle it, stroke it, press the right buttons and blow into it until it squealed with pleasure. Recently Rhona had noticed a difference. She had begun to suspect that Sean was not playing her any more, he was playing with her, an entirely different thing.

'Good?' Sean said.

'Delicious.'

'I put the pasta in the fridge. It'll do for tomorrow night.'

Sean played a regular gig in a club in the centre of town every Friday night. The Ultimate Jazz Club was dark and intimate. On Fridays it was always packed. The gig started at ten o'clock and didn't finish till two. Sean often stayed there jamming until sunrise. Rhona had loved to watch him play, ever since the night they met. He'd been booked to play at a police function at the club. At the interval he'd come over to her table and asked if he could talk to her. He was so straightforward, she couldn't refuse. Besides, she'd been having erotic thoughts about him all evening. She stayed on till late, till the band wound down, playing soft soul music while the crowd drifted off. After he'd packed up his gear, they'd left together and they'd been together ever since.

I can't go back to the club, she thought. Not now I know.

Sean was up, whistling as he rattled cups and spooned freshly ground coffee into the machine.

'I went to the Art Gallery on Friday,' Rhona heard herself say in a detached voice.

Sean didn't answer at first and she wondered whether he had been listening. Often when he whistled he was miles away, planning a tune in his head. Not this time. This time he heard her.

He brought the cafetière over to the table and poured the coffee. He was whistling again, bringing the notes to a proper end before he spoke.

'Ordinary people go to art galleries here. I like that. It reminds me of Dublin.'

His voice was unperturbed and soothing. He was not going to be drawn into a sparring match. They lapsed into silence. Rhona fingered her cup.

'You were in the Gallery on Friday,' she said.

'I was.'

(Was that a question or an answer?)

'You were with a woman,' she said.

'I was.'

He took a sip of coffee then placed his cup gently back on the saucer. He did everything like that, his big hands moving in firm gentle ways.

'Who was she?' Rhona tried to make her voice as if she didn't care.

Sean studied her carefully, his eyes catching hers.

'A woman I know who likes art galleries,' he said.

'Like me.'

'No,' he shook his head, 'not like you.' He ran his fingers through his hair.

I've got to him, she thought. She waited for him to say something else, then interrupted him when he tried.

'Rhona . . .'

'Are you fucking her?'

'Fucking her?' He repeated the words so lightly they no longer seemed important. 'It doesn't matter if I am.'

'It matters to me,' she said angrily.

He didn't answer. In the distance Rhona heard a church clock chime. She counted eight before he spoke.

'That's because you make it matter,' he said quietly.

Sean was never outright angry. When he was ruffled or irritated he always gave the impression he couldn't understand what all the fuss was about. Sometimes Rhona wished he would argue with her, let it out. But he never did and she was always left yapping at his heels like a terrier.

'If I tell you I'm not, will you believe me?' he said.

She had known this would happen.

'Listen.' He reached over the table and lifted her chin and made her look at him. 'I will not cook for her or play for her or stroke the back of her neck when she's tired,' and he ran his hand tenderly down the curve of her face.

They left the table without clearing it and moved through to the living room. Sean lit the gas fire and closed the curtains. He sat on the couch and made a place for her in the crook of his arm. Rhona allowed herself to slip close against him, laying her head on his chest; already thinking of what her life would be like without him.

When the phone rang, Sean was the one who got up and answered it.

'It's for you,' he said. 'A man. Didn't give his name.' Sean's face betrayed nothing.

She took the receiver and Sean left the room. From the bedroom she heard a trickle of notes.

'Hello?'

'Rhona? It's Edward. Edward Stewart.' The repetition was unnecessary. As if Rhona wouldn't know that voice anywhere, at any time.

There was the sound of a throat being cleared.

'Would it be possible to speak to you about some business?'

'No.'

'Rhona, this is difficult for me . . .'

Things were always difficult for him, never for anyone else.

'Fuck off, Edward,' she said and began to put the phone down.

'Rhona, wait, please. It's important.'

There was something in his voice that stopped her.

'Could we meet?' he was asking.

Rhona heard herself agree.

'Tomorrow. Half ten?'

Edward was confident again as he said good-bye. He's got what he wanted, she thought. What sort of business could he possibly want to discuss? Business, as in his law firm, or business as in the by-election he's hoping to win next month? And why now, she asked herself. We haven't spoken in three years, and then only across a bench in court. He hadn't been pleased when her evidence put his client away. Edward didn't like losing.

Sean was still playing his saxophone but now he'd moved to a tune that Rhona had come to think of as theirs. The tune he'd been playing, he said, when he fell in love with her.

She knew he meant it now as a peace offering.

Sean wouldn't ask her who the man on the phone was. He wouldn't ask her if she'd slept with him in the past or was sleeping with him in the present. He wouldn't ask because it wouldn't make any difference to the way he felt about her.

Rhona only wished she could feel the same.

4

THERE WERE TIMES when Bill Wilson thought he had been in the police force too long. Such negative thoughts usually surfaced when Margaret, his wife, told him off for talking to their two teenage children 'like you're interrogating them', or when (like last night) he'd told an unmarked police car to follow his daughter, Lisa, home from a club. It was ironic, really. After this latest murder he should have asked the patrol to follow his son Robbie home instead. Either child would hit the roof, if they found out. Having a policeman father had never been easy. When Lisa complained he was over-protective, he could only say, 'I'm a man. I know how men think.'

It was part of his job to climb into sick minds. If his family had been able to see what he was thinking half the time, Bill suspected they would have packed up and left him years ago.

When he'd told Rhona MacLeod that he thought the latest victim was a regular rent boy, though higher class than usual, he'd been wrong. The boy wasn't known in the Glasgow rent scene at all and it was beginning to look as if he couldn't have been a runaway. If he had been on the game, it couldn't have been for long.

Just long enough to end up dead.

He stared at the photograph on his desk. Most photos taken in booths were done for a laugh. Two or three faces pressed together in a moment of hilarity, eyes reddened by the flash.

This photograph wasn't like that.

The boy had positioned himself carefully for the camera. He was smartly dressed in a buttoned up shirt with a small collar and a dark blue jacket. His thick, curly hair had refused to be tamed for the picture and it flopped over his eyes, making him look very vulnerable. And there was no mistaking it. The set of the jaw, the neat nose, those eyes. The resemblance to Rhona was inescapable.

Bill leaned back in the old leather chair he hadn't let them throw out when they refurbished his office. In this chair he could think, even if the Super thought it screwed up the décor.

He felt sure that this was no regular rent boy. Trussed up in death in that sordid little flat he hadn't looked streetwise, and he didn't look streetwise in this photo. Why would he have wanted a photograph like this? Bill thought about his own son. Sixteen years old and not half as civilised looking. Why would Robbie want such a formal picture? Maybe for an identity card?

He sat up and pressed the button on his desk. After a few insistent buzzes, the door opened and DC Clarke stuck her head round.

'Check the universities and colleges, Janice. Ask if any of their students have gone AWOL.'

'You think he might have been a student stuck for cash?'

They'd already cautioned a student newspaper for advertising jobs in a local sauna to 'willing young female students needing extra cash'. The editor had withdrawn the advert but was unrepentant. As far as he was concerned, it was a legit way to pay for an education.

'Go and see the editor of that student paper. See if they've had any requests to place adverts for willing young boys.'

Janice raised her eyebrows in distaste.

'And get Dr MacLeod on the phone for me. Maybe she's found something that might help confirm this line of enquiry.'

But Dr MacLeod was not available.

'Chrissy says she left two hours ago and hasn't come back yet. Went to meet some mysterious man with a sexy voice.'

'Constable . . .'

'Chrissy's words, Sir, not mine. They'll get back to us later about any results.'

It didn't matter what day it was or what time of day, the Kelvingrove Art Gallery and Museum was always busy. This morning there was a class in from Glasgow School of Art. The students were clustered on and around the south steps leading up from the main hall, sketch pads on their knees. The grand hall was beautiful, Rhona thought, each layer a work of art in itself. A series of statues gazed down from the first floor balcony; smooth white marble forms that Rhona stroked as a child. Early spring sunshine filtered through the stained glass windows, dancing rainbows over the dark polished wood.

A group from a primary school was weaving towards the dinosaur room. Rhona wandered after them and watched them gaze up in awe at the reconstructed skeletons. A wee blond boy was standing apart from the others, squinting through a microscope at the fossilised remains of a mosquito that had been trapped for eternity in tree sap turned into amber. Jurassic Park comes to Glasgow, she thought. And what did that matter, if it made the child think and ask questions?

Rhona's father had often brought her here and as they'd wandered together through the endless rooms she'd asked him hundreds of questions. Her Dad answered every one of them. He'd made most of it up, she knew that now, but it didn't matter because his interest and sense of wonder had been real, and he'd passed that on to her.

Edward, Rhona knew, would be on time and so she had arrived early to compose herself. When she was with him she always had the feeling he was trying to manipulate her, get her to do what he wanted. Even after all these years, he might still be able to make her feel inadequate. In court it was different. There, she was discussing facts. She could weigh them objectively, make rational decisions. Edward could not unnerve her there.

She left the wee boy squatting below the genetic pattern of the dinosaur, pencilling in his jotter, and headed for the café. She wanted to be sitting there when Edward arrived.

Edward Stewart turned into the car park, cutting abruptly across the path of a battered red Mini. He regretted it almost immediately when a quick glance showed the driver to be an attractive young woman. He slowed down and gave her a friendly, apologetic wave, hoping to give the impression his mind had been elsewhere (which it had), and was rewarded with a dazzling smile.

There were very few cars in the car park but he knew that didn't mean the Gallery was empty. He could only hope there wouldn't be a horde of noisy school kids around when he met Rhona. Perhaps this wasn't the ideal venue for what he had to say.

He pulled up and waited for a moment before he switched off, taking pleasure in the easy purr of the big engine, then he glanced in the rear view mirror. He admired his tan, the result of a fortnight in Paxos with Fiona. He smoothed back his hair, adjusted the knot on the new Italian silk tie he'd awarded himself for the Giuliano case, and gave himself a confident smile. Think positive, he told himself. That's what gets results.

He climbed out, pointed the remote at the car and waited for the satisfying click. He had already decided that he would tell Rhona just enough and no more; he would rely on her need for privacy and her integrity. Both, he knew from experience, were reliable.

The main hall confirmed his worst fears. The place

was swarming with primary kids studying the exhibits. He glanced at his watch. Ten twenty-five. Thirty-five minutes before this lot would descend on the café for crisps and Coca Cola.

Edward spotted Rhona and was momentarily non-plussed. It would have been a point of advantage for him to have been there first. To be able to look up on her arrival, smile, stand up. Rhona was normally late. He had assumed that.

It was then she glanced round and saw him. The sound of her voice calling his name made his stomach contract. He put on a bright smile and walked forward. As always, he imagined what he must look like as he approached her and made instant small adjustments to improve the picture. He brushed her cheek lightly with his lips. 'It's great to see you,' he said.

The lie was not lost on her and he immediately regretted his choice of opening remark. He tried to retrieve the situation.

'Can I get you anything?'

She shook her head.

Edward headed for the counter, annoyed to find the confidence of the tan and the silk tie evaporating.

Rhona was waiting for him to speak, her face ex-pressionless. It was the look she wore when she knew he was going to ask her to do something. The look he had always striven to change, by fair means or foul. Today was no exception.

When the constituency secretary phoned him and offered him the candidacy, Edward felt like punching the air and shouting, 'Ya beauty'. It was what his kids might have done. Instead he said yes, walked through to the sitting room, poured two large whiskies and gave one to Fiona. She accepted it without a word and raised it high in the air. The triumph was no less hers. It was what she wanted too. Jonathan and Morag were both upstairs, but they didn't call them down to tell them. Teenagers did not, could not, understand the significance of such an event.

They sat together that evening, basking in mutual congratulation, refilling their whisky glasses and discussing the implications. The seat he was offered was a promising one. There was no doubt about that. There were few seats in Scotland that they would be likely to hold on to, and this was one of them. If all went well, Edward's future was assured. He would be less involved with his law work, that was true. But he had planned ahead. He was already on a number of company boards and his knowledge of European law brought in consultancy work. Becoming an MP would only serve to enhance the comfortable life Edward Stewart had created for himself.

Rhona had waited long enough.

'Well?'

'It was good of you to come,' Edward began.

'Cut the small talk, Edward. I'm not a future constituent. You and I both know that you wouldn't have asked me here unless it was absolutely necessary.' Her voice was rigid with emotion.

She watched his face tense up momentarily, then

readjust into something more pleasant. Whatever speech he had planned for her was being seriously rewritten.

'So?' she said.

'Okay, okay. Give me a chance.'

She waited.

'I asked you to come here this morning because,' a pause here – an attempt at sincerity, 'I need your help.'

Silence, then her own incredulous voice.

'You need *my* help?'

She was making him squirm, and she had to admit she was enjoying it. Edward looked as though he might give up on the whole thing, then he marshalled himself.

'There's no reason why we shouldn't keep in touch. After all, we were once very close.'

'Not any more.'

'That wasn't my fault.' His voice had acquired a petulant tone. 'If you remember, you walked out on me.'

'Shortly after I came home to find you using the flat for a lunchtime fuck. Your legal secretary, wasn't it?'

'If I had to look elsewhere for affection . . .' he began reproachfully.

'Don't you dare blame that on me.' Her heart was thumping now. This was ridiculous. She was arguing about something that happened donkey's years ago. She got up.

'No, please don't.' He put his hand on her arm. 'You're right of course.' His voice was apologetic. 'It was all my fault.'

Rhona sat down again, emotionally exhausted. She would let Edward have his say and go.

'After all, you were ill,' he continued, searching for the right words, 'because of the incident.'

She looked at him, puzzled.

'I should have made allowances, but I needed . . .'

'Sex?'

He was annoyed. 'Company. You would hardly speak to me, let alone . . . anyway that's what I wanted to talk to you about.'

'Your sex drive?'

He cleared his throat. 'That's not funny, Rhona. I am referring to the incident, of course.'

'The incident?' she repeated in disbelief. The feeling of hysteria that Edward had generated in her was changing to depression. Edward couldn't possibly mean what she thought he meant. The incident? Of course. What else would Edward call it? But she still had to ask. Had to make sure.

'What incident?'

He ignored her question, which could only mean one thing. She was right. He began again, his voice a little firmer this time. She found herself concentrating on his mouth, out of which that word had come.

'I wanted to speak to you before the by-election,' he was explaining.

Rhona stared over his shoulder. The little boy from the dinosaur room was heading towards the café. He looked excited, clutching an open jotter in his hand. His teacher bent to look at his drawing, giving quiet words of praise.

'Rhona?' Edward's voice was tinged with annoyance.

'Why are you bringing this up now, Edward? It was seventeen years ago,' she said, not trusting herself to look at him.

'You know what the press is like.' His voice had a jocular tone now. 'A story like that about a prospective MP.' He laughed a little. 'And I wouldn't like your privacy to be violated.'

'My privacy!'

The words exploded from her and the school party at the next table fell silent, with the awkwardness of children in the vicinity of an adult argument. Edward looked uncomfortable, then pulled himself together and smiled vaguely. His discomfort, she sensed, had turned to intense irritation. She had often irritated him, she remembered. Whenever she had seemed 'over-emotional', as he put it.

'I have to get back,' she said, standing up and looking at her watch.

'Right.' He stood up beside her and spoke firmly as if the end of the meeting had been decided by him. 'I'll walk through the park with you.'

'No you won't.'

He stepped back, surprised.

'Goodbye, Edward. And Edward, don't contact me again . . . ever.'

5

RHONA LEFT THE Gallery by the double doors hoping they would swing back and slap Edward right in his condescending face. She should have known better. The incident! How could he talk about Liam like that?

Rhona headed towards Kelvingrove Park. At her back the children from the primary school were laughing and screaming as they ran down the steps and headed for their bus. Rhona turned quickly down the avenue of trees towards the river, shutting out the sound of their laughter. When she reached the bridge, she stopped, breathless. Below, the water moved sluggishly between banks of bracken. She leaned on the metal rail, watching the muddy swirl, and let herself remember.

It was the morning they'd taken Liam away. The nurse had given her a pill to stop the milk coming through. Her nipples were painfully tender against her nightdress, making dark circles in the white cotton. Liam was lying in the cot beside her, washed and changed. She reached over and touched his face. The blue-veined eyelids quivered and the small mouth began to suck at nothing. She remembered the shape of him, the long legs curled up when she wanted to change him, the folds of skin waiting to be filled. They had told her he was perfect. She wasn't to worry about the birthmark, a strawberry-shaped lump on the inside of his right leg. It would fade.

When she first told Edward she was pregnant, he had been kind. He had put his arm round her and she had nestled into him, feeling his heart thumping in his chest. He was trying to work out what the hell to do next. She knew he would not want the baby. She was nineteen, he was twenty-one. He had just graduated. A law firm had already grabbed him.

He chose his words carefully. It was the beginning of their life together, he said. They weren't ready for a baby. She had to finish her degree. Do her PhD. She thought she felt the same way. She didn't want a baby. She wanted a career. And that's what she got.

Edward never even came to the hospital (it was better that way, he explained). Edward had never seen his son at all.

Rhona could hardly bear the memory of it all. This had not happened to her for a long time. This thinking and feeling. Thinking about stuff that could never be changed. And the guilt. She looked in her pocket for something to wipe her eyes. She should have stayed away from him. Well away. Even professionally their paths rarely crossed. Edward was not a criminal lawyer. Crimes of passion were not his style. They were too messy. Like having a baby at the wrong time.

Rhona sat down on a bench. An old man looked round as if he was going to speak to her, so she coughed into her hankie and wiped her nose as he muttered something about the rain being on its way. Thank God, she thought, for the shitey Scottish fucking weather. At least if it rains, no one will see me cry.

And it did. Above her the clouds rolled in, thick and grey. She watched as it speckled round her feet, felt the drops fall singly on her head, then in multiples. She got up and began to walk, holding her face up to the downpour.

When she got back to the lab, there was a message for her on the desk. She looked guiltily at the clock above the door. Two o'clock. She must have been wandering about for hours. She hung up her wet coat and went and washed her face and combed her hair, then sat down at her desk.

The message on the pad was brief. Rhona could smell annoyance in the sweep of the pen and the final period that threatened to pierce the paper. Chrissy was peeved about her disappearance, when there was 'urgent work to be done'. She had had to go over to the chemistry lab with some flakes of paint she'd found in the jacket pocket and she hadn't had a chance to start on the semen stains. And DC Clarke had called looking for results.

Rhona settled down to do the work she should have been doing instead of listening to Edward patronise her. Chrissy had meticulously entered the results from her tests in the lab notebook. The rest was in her notes. She'd examined the boy's clothes in detail and taken samples from the collar and cuffs of his jacket for DNA purposes. Everything was standard teenage wear that could be bought in a variety of shops throughout the country and so unlikely to help them find out who he was. She had found some fibres on the jeans which still had to be analysed. She had also established the boy's blood group from the sample taken from his arm the previous night and compared it to the large bloodstain on the bed. There was no surprise in the match. The boy was type A, as were approximately forty-two per cent of the UK population. As for semen and other blood samples on the cover, there was a lot of material still to cover. Oh, and Dr Sissons had sent round the silk cord for them to examine. He had finished with it now that he'd established the cause of death.

Rhona sat down at the comparison microscope to check the control hair she'd taken from the boy's head against the two hairs (dark and blond) she'd found on his body. Proving hairs to be from the same person was tricky. Proving them to be from different people was easier. Through the eyepiece, the two hairs side by side looked like two sections of a tree trunk, patterned and grained. In the control hair the bark was smooth, in the other the bark was significantly shredded. Cuticles, cortex and medulla of the darker hair were all significantly different. She then examined the blond hair and was surprised to find similar differences. At first sight, neither of the hairs belonged to the victim. Of course, he might have picked them up from sharing a towel, but one of them might belong to the murderer.

Rhona felt the shiver of pleasure she always got when the pieces of the jigsaw began to fit together. The DNA lab could derive a profile from a single human hair. That and the semen might be all they would need to place a murderer at the scene of the crime.

The DNA profile would be sent to the Scottish National Database in Dundee. If they didn't find a match, then it would be sent south to the National Database. If the murderer wasn't on either of them, they would have to find him some other way.

It would be difficult to pinpoint the exact time it happened. Probably there wasn't an exact time at all. Lots of times during that hour, as she pored over her microscope, the thought flirted with Rhona, that somewhere out there she had a child. A son. A boy of her own. Like the wee boy in the museum. The wee boy with the blond hair. But no, she reminded herself. Her son wouldn't be writing about dinosaurs in a jotter in large round letters and running to show his teacher. Her son had done all that years ago. That was all gone. Seventeen years of a life, somewhere. A life she had missed. Her son was almost a man.

Rhona left the microscope and went over to the bench where Chrissy had spread out the photographs from the murder scene like a bizarre tablecloth. She picked one up and stared at it. It was a close up of the welts on the neck. The lens had caught the curve of the cheek and the right eye. The eyelashes seemed improbably long and curled, a dark blond fringe above the empty stare.

The Sergeant had said the boy looked so like her, he might have been her brother. Maybe even her son? Rhona selected the photographs that contained his face and placed them in a row to study them in more detail, trying to ignore the grotesque pose, the patchwork skin, the blank eyes. Would her son look like the boy in the photo? They would be about the same age. He would have blond hair (she and Edward were both fair), possibly curly, like hers. He would be tall, his eyes blue, the lashes darker than the hair. She imagined his face. Longish. A smile like Edward's, but true. A smile that would shine in his eyes. Rhona pushed the photographs to one side.

The telephone shattered her mental image of her son's smiling face. It broke into fragments, then re-formed, but this time it was the other face, the one that lay on the dirty pillow, twisted sideways, the blond hair damp against the forehead, the blue eyes wide and cold, the neck a welt of pain.

'Rhona. Is that you?'

It was Sean. She heard her voice methodically answer his questions. Yes, she was fine. Yes, she would come to the gig tonight if he really wanted her to.

Anything would be better than being left alone to think.

'You sure you're okay?' he asked again.

'Of course, I'm fine. I'm sorry, Sean, I'll have to go.'

'I'll pick you up at five then. We can eat out.'

'No. I can't. I mean, I don't know when I'll get finished here,' she lied. 'We're short-staffed.'

Sean sounded disappointed and Rhona immediately felt bad. Guilt was her middle name, she thought.

'I'll see you after, then,' Sean said.

'Right.'

That was the problem, she thought. The problem

with Sean. She didn't tell him anything. Well, not anything important. What she really thought. What she really felt. Oh, he knew her. Quite well in fact. He knew her moods. Sean was good with moods. He could spot them from a great distance and adjust himself accordingly. He could always make her laugh when she was mad or sad. Unlike her, Sean was never in a mood. Or he was always in the same one.

She should have agreed to let him come at five. She glanced up at the clock. No. It would have been too soon. She wasn't ready to face him. She wasn't ready to face anyone yet. She couldn't think about Sean just now. There was too much to do. When she was working, she didn't have time to think about anything, except the samples. Samples of other people's lives, other people's mistakes, other people's crimes.

Chrissy did not come back all afternoon. She called at four to apologise and ask if she could come in late next day.

'I know it's a bad time, I wouldn't ask but . . .'

Something was obviously still wrong at home. Since Patrick moved out, Chrissy had carried both the financial and the emotional burden of her family. And if her father had his way, Patrick would never come back, even to visit. But Chrissy knew that would break her mother's heart, so at home she was forever smoothing troubled waters.

'It's okay. It's time I did some of the work myself. I'll see you some time tomorrow.'

Chrissy murmured her thanks and hung up.

Rhona worked until seven then tidied the lab and

left. Outside it was tipping down. She headed for the front of the Gallery, hoping to spot a taxi near Kelvinhall. She put up her umbrella but within minutes her legs and feet were soaked and heavy drops fell from the spokes and whipped back into her face. There was one taxi at the rank and she ran for it, dodging cars. A bus, its windscreen wipers battling the onslaught, braked as she darted in front of it. Her dice with death was pointless. When she got to the other side, the taxi had already taken off, swooping round in a wide circle to answer a wave from behind.

Rhona swore loudly. She was on her third staccato 'Fuck' when the taxi drew up beside her and the door swung open.

'Need a lift?'

Rhona glared into the cab. The driver grinned out at her, as did the man in the back. A flush began to creep up her neck.

'Sorry. I just wanted to get home.'

The man's smile grew wider. 'If you don't mind sharing we can give the driver a double fare.'

'Thanks.'

He held the door open for her while she got inside. She sat the dripping brolly between them, then felt guilty when she noticed his wet trouser leg and shifted it to the other side. They moved a little closer together. She could smell him now. A mixture of damp wool and aftershave.

'Where to?' he asked.

'Atholl Crescent.'

He leaned forward and spoke to the driver, who

seemed to find the whole thing amusing. Rhona surreptitiously wiped her nose on her sleeve.

'We'll let you off first,' her fellow occupant suggested, and she nodded.

They drew to a halt at a set of lights and she took the opportunity to have a better look at her rescuer. He was tall. She was conscious of the length of his legs beside her. His hair was blond, darkened by the rain. He knew she was looking at him and he turned and smiled.

'Water all over the road,' the driver informed them. 'The gutter can't take this amount of rain.'

'Typical Scottish summer,' her companion remarked.

The rain was sweeping across the Victorian façade of the University and lightning forked above the Philosophy Tower.

'The Hammer House of Horror,' her rescuer suggested mildly, following her gaze.

'That's where I work.'

'Oh, sorry.'

Rhona shook her head. 'It is the Hammer House of Horror at times,' she said.

He inclined his head as if he was going to ask her what she did, and then seemed to change his mind. So she volunteered the information herself. He didn't make a funny remark. She liked him for that.

'So you work with the police department?' he said. She nodded.

'That's funny. So do I. Different area, of course. Computing.'

When the taxi finally drew up in front of her building

Rhona didn't want to get out. She felt relaxed sharing a taxi with this stranger, painting a picture of her life that sounded interesting, that contained none of the awkward bits, the bits that needed explaining.

'Well, here we are,' he said and leaned over to click open her door.

She climbed out and opened her bag, searching for her purse.

'No. Let me. It was on my way, anyway.'

He looked at her for a moment and their eyes held.

'See you,' he said.

'See you.'

The door slammed behind her. She didn't bother putting the brolly up and by the time she crossed the pavement and got to the front door, her hair was soaking. She rummaged in her bag again, this time for her key, but before she could put it in the lock, the buzzer went and the door was free.

'Saw you from the window,' Sean's voice came from the speaker.

Rhona pushed open the door and went inside.

6

IT ALL SOUNDED too far-fetched and Bill Wilson couldn't get his head round it at first. The woman who was talking to them seemed genuine enough, but Bill had long experience of social workers and he didn't like them on principle. It wasn't anything personal. He just got fed up with the excuses. Excuses why people did this and didn't do that, as if no one was responsible for their own behaviour any more. It seemed people did bad things nowadays because they were unhappy as children. Bill Wilson thought that was a load of shite. When he was wee, children had had plenty to be miserable about, if money had anything to do with it. Money had been the scarcest commodity on his street, but hard graft and hard knocks hadn't turned people into the creeps this woman was talking about.

The course had been going on all afternoon. Bill had said he was too busy to go and suggested sending two of the team along instead, but the Super had said no. He had to go himself. Something this woman was going to say might help with the latest murder and he wanted Bill there.

The first hour had been all the routine stuff on sexual abuse a rookie needed to know. Bill had heard it all before. It didn't upset him the way it had his neighbour. He guessed Constable McPhail must have a young child. By the end, she had a look on her face that said, 'I just want to go home and hold my kid.'

For the last hour they'd moved upstairs from the conference room to a computer lab. There were three people working in there, a woman and two men. Bill had the feeling that if the Constable felt bad before, she was going to feel a whole lot worse after this session.

The project had been going for about three months, the child abuse worker explained. It was pretty easy to find porn on the Internet but it was harder to track down where the material was coming from. Then there were the chat rooms. Most of them were no worse or better than the telephone chat lines advertised in a lot of newspapers. These weren't their main concern, either.

In the space of seconds, the woman was saying, you could look at anything that took your fancy. And she gave them a demo just to show that what she said was true. The photos appearing on the screen were high resolution. Clear pictures of the frightened faces of children forced into an ugly adult world they should have been protected from.

Bill took a look at his neighbour. Constable McPhail looked almost as frightened and bewildered as the children in the pictures, but the child abuse worker never flinched. She walked between the consoles, pointing out references and web addresses, linking the patterns to show how the threads that made up the awful net of corruption wound straight back to Scotland.

They believed there were three paedophile rings operating in Glasgow, she explained. All three were separate but in contact with one another. New technology offered a fast track to new recruitment.

Imagine a child at the computer, she said. A quiet child, perhaps a bit of a loner. An adolescent boy. This boy liked using the Internet. He could talk to others with the same interests as himself, without ever having to meet them. He could be a bit more open than usual in these electronic conversations, a bit more adventurous. He could give himself a new name, a new persona. It was every awkward child's idea of Heaven. Not that different from ringing up a sex line number, she said, and there was an uneasy laugh from a couple of men at the back. Bill didn't join in and neither did Constable McPhail.

It didn't take long for a paedophile ring to compile a list of possibilities and then the courtship began. Much like any other courtship. Just friendly at first, finding a mutual interest to talk about. There were lots of chat rooms on the Internet, the woman explained, and for good measure she showed them one.

The name of the chat room generated some tentative laughter. Bill could see the guys were uneasy at being reminded that 95 per cent of all sexual abuse was perpetrated by men.

Fortunately *Busty Blondes* turned out to be a joke. It centred mainly on pictures of Pamela Anderson's tits and what you thought about them, in minute detail. The likelihood was, the woman was saying, that someone was wanking off to this right at this minute. There was no shortage of customers. This particular chat room was full.

Once a child was identified, they got started in earnest. Kids often logged on at night or in the early hours of the morning when their parents were asleep. After the 'I am your friend' conversations, the pictures would arrive. Not bad at first, the usual girlie stuff. She gave the room a look that said, *just like the ones we've all just laughed at.* The sort of stuff it would be embarrassing for an adolescent to buy over the counter. If the kid responded, then the next set would be more horny, might shock them a little, but always the reassurance that there was no harm in it. After all it was on the television all the time.

There were a few uncomfortable blokes in that room by now. Bill could sense them. No one liked the idea that anything they did or watched or looked at led to this.

Then the next set of pictures would arrive. Things the kid might think about but never dare ask to see. Things that shocked but made you go back for more. If the kid stayed on line, the paedos were made. If the kid logged off, then it wasn't over yet. There was always the threat of blackmail. They would threaten to send some of the messages to the child's parents, maybe some of the pictures. Either way, they had the child hooked.

The next step was the meeting. Then the abuse could begin in earnest.

Bill stood on the steps of the University and took a deep breath. He wanted to clear his head of the stink.

Constable McPhail was coming down the steps behind him. She gave him a look that said she'd had enough for one day and headed for her car. He took a split-second decision not to go back to the office right away. He needed fresh air, the normality of people walking about, shopping, living. People who couldn't do things like that to children. He turned and walked towards the park. The trees were fresh green, the delicate green you get in Scotland in early summer. The rain had washed the street and the deep gutters were running with water from the heavy showers. He walked at a steady pace, planting his feet firmly as if there had to be something in this life that was solid and believable. As he passed Gilmorehill the big double doors swung open and the students poured out, desperate to get out of the exam hall and away. Some were talking excitedly, hysterical with the need to unburden how bad it had been. Others couldn't talk about it at all.

Bill was not a man to talk for the sake of it either. There were bits of today he would rather forget. He headed down through the park towards the River Kelvin. A wee girl was playing all alone on the grass. She must have been about eight. He walked more slowly, hoping her mother would appear, or a big sister or brother. He hesitated when the path remained empty, wondering whether he should go over and ask her where she lived. He sat down on a bench and waited, suddenly conscious that he looked like a loi-terer himself. A middle-aged man sitting watching a wee lassie playing on the grass. At last a woman came up the steep path from the river and shouted crossly, grabbing the girl by the hand and wrenching her off. Bill breathed a sigh of relief.

He knew all about this. The heightened awareness, the worry. After every murder or violent crime it was the same. For a while he desperately wanted to protect all the vulnerable and the innocent.

He suddenly realised how close he was to Rhona's lab. He hadn't spoken to her since he'd warned her about the press. Now he could tell her a little more about the victim. At least they had a distinguishing mark.

7

THE FLAT WAS big and friendly. Rhona had fallen in love with it three years ago and when she moved in, she spent the first three weeks saying out loud, 'I love this flat'. Then, there had been no one there to hear her or to think she was going mad. Just the cat, and the cat didn't listen to her anyway. When the woman had opened the door the night she went to view, Rhona had known right away that this was going to be her home. Not even the dreich Glasgow night had dampened her enthusiasm. She had vowed to herself and the cat that she would allow no one, no one to encroach on their living space. And she had kept her word, until Sean.

Early evening light was entering the kitchen, touching the worktops with a warm, golden glow. The golden colour came from the convent tucked behind them, its carefully tended garden a tribute to order and faith. Tonight the toll of the bell for worship only reminded Rhona that she had no faith, in God or in herself, any more.

She had come home shortly after DI Wilson left the laboratory. There had been something achingly sad about his pleasure in revealing the information on the birthmark. She could feel her face freeze as he explained that it was just a raised area on the boy's inside right thigh. But when he was a baby, he said, it would have been more obvious. It might help them identify him.

The silent scream was still there. Seventeen years on and it was still there. She had sat on the bus home, hearing it echo through her brain. She had actually begun to shake, and the woman beside her asked what the problem was and whether she needed a doctor.

As soon as she got to the flat, she shut the door and locked it before she made the call. She knew it would achieve nothing, but she had to make it all the same. The hospital gave her a further number which they said might be able to help. They warned how difficult it might be. An adopted child could not be forced to contact a natural parent. The adoptive parents might not agree, either.

Grief has the ability to strip away time. Rhona had felt it when her father died. Looking down at his still face, it was as if her own adult life dissolved, leaving her a wee girl again. A girl whose hand fitted easily inside his big one, whose cheek met his in a whiff of tobacco smoke and bristly beard. All her certainties began to crumble. And it was happening again. Seventeen years of her life dissolving into nothingness.

There was a knock at the door, then a second, much louder, then someone tried the lock, rasping it this way and that. Her name was being called. It came from far away.

'Rhona. It's me, Sean. Open the door.'

She went to the door and unlocked it.

'Sorry,' she said. 'I must have turned the key by mistake.' She kept her face away from him because she had no idea what she looked like. She didn't even know if she'd been crying.

Rhona went into the kitchen. The golden light was still there, trying to lift the room to normality. She went to the fridge, took out a bottle of wine and opened it.

Sean didn't like drama. She knew that. He was puzzled by it. His attitude to life was, if things went wrong, they went wrong. If he couldn't figure out why, he forgot about it and went and played his music. Music held all the drama Sean needed. Tonight he didn't go and play his saxophone, but followed her into the kitchen.

'I'm going away for a week,' he said quietly. He poured himself a glass of wine and sat down opposite her at the table. 'I've got a gig in Paris.'

She said nothing and he reached out and took her hand, stroking the palm gently with his thumb. 'An old mate of mine wants me to fill a spot while one of the band takes a holiday.' He gripped her hand more tightly now and dipped his head so that he caught her eyes and drew them up to meet his.

'I thought you might come with me.'

'I can't.'

'Why not?'

'The murder . . .'

'You'll have finished with that. I don't go for a couple of days yet.'

She shook her head. 'No, it'll take longer.'

She pulled her hand away. The convent bells had

stopped and the world seemed suddenly empty with-out them. If she refused to go with Sean to Paris he might not come back, at least not to the flat, not to her. She could not let herself think about that, not just now.

He caught her arm as she made for the door.

'You're going to have to tell me if you don't want me, Rhona. You're going to have to say the words.' He laid his cheek against hers and spoke softly in her ear. 'Tell me, Rhona. Tell me you want me to go away. Tell me you don't want me to come back.'

In the silence that followed he moved his mouth to cover hers.

When Bill got back to the office after speaking to Rhona, he found his desk plastered with yellow note-lets. It seemed as though plenty had been happening while he was away. According to Janice, the owner of the murder flat was swanning his time away in a bar he owned in Tenerife. The guy had lots of money and plenty of property in and around Glasgow, most of the details of which were well hidden. The flat in question was let out for him by a property services company on Dumbarton Road. Janice had already been there. The place was clean-looking, she reported, but deserted. Maybe the owners had also decided to take a break.

Rhona had brought him up to date on the forensic results.

'We've identified a DNA profile from the saliva and the seminal fluid. We also have two hairs, neither of which came from the boy,' she said.

'So we have a genetic profile of the killer?'

'Yes. I've sent the samples to the DNA lab. The fastest they can do is forty-eight hours.'

'It's not much use without a suspect,' he said.

'Maybe we'll be lucky with the DNA database.'

'Let's hope so. What about the cover?'

'There are a number of older stains still to examine.'

'The cover's had a busy time of it then?' he said.

'Yes. I'm afraid it has.'

DC Clarke told him the cover was even more interesting than that. They were now sure it had been a curtain, made to measure by the looks of it, and expensive. So it was possible the material might be traceable. The pattern was very distinctive, huge swirls of red, blue and green silk.

Bill thought back to that terrible room. The smell of sex and sweat and dirt and those awful shite coloured curtains pulled tightly across the window to hide what went on inside.

'The material is French,' Janice was saying. 'We even have the maker's name.' She almost smiled. 'A small but exclusive shop in the rue St George near the Sacré Coeur stocks it. We think someone either bought the material in this country from an imported lot and had the curtains made up, or they bought it in Paris. Either way it can be traced, Sir.'

Bill was pleased.

'Better contact the Procurator Fiscal's office, and get permission to release details on the curtain in case someone recognises it.'

'Done that already, Sir,' Janice declared triumphantly.

It seemed the ship ran quite smoothly without him.
'How did the course go?' she asked.
'Grim.'
She'd guessed as much already, she said. She'd
spoken to Constable McPhail. Apparently she'd
decided to go home straight afterwards and see her
wee girl.
'Aye. I don't blame her,' Bill agreed.
They said when you stopped caring about what
happened to people in this job, it was time to retire.
Bill wondered just what level of caring was supporta-
ble. It was a bit like being a doctor. Care enough but
not too much, not so you took it home. He'd survived
in this business a long time. He could still laugh when
things got rough. You had to have a sense of humour or
you'd go mad, as mad as the folk you were trying to
catch and lock up.
The problem was, he'd lost his sense of humour on
this one. This crime had become too personal somehow. And something in Rhona's face when he told her
about the boy's birthmark had unnerved him. It was
the same expression he'd seen on the face of the young
female Constable at the Child Abuse course; haunted,
guilty, despairing, as if the world was too horrible a
place to live in.
When he'd arrived at the lab, Rhona had been
working at her desk and she hadn't tied her hair back.
It was loose about her face, making her look too young,
like a student, rather than the experienced scientist Bill
knew she was. When he told her about the birthmark,
he knew his voice had been excited because he wanted

to believe that they had something to go on, something that would help them identify the boy. And Rhona's face had crumpled. Someone other than himself was taking this murder to heart.

The phone rang. It was McSween.

'You asked for word on those glasses.'

'Mmm.'

'Fingerprints show one was used by the boy, the other by an unknown.'

'Right.'

'And Sir . . .'

'What?'

'They were drinking good whisky, Sir. The Big T, it's called. Origin, Tomatin Distillery, Invernesshire.'

The boy, it seemed, had drunk well before he died on his designer curtain.

Bill looked at his watch. He'd been told to be home sharp tonight. Margaret had organised a meal out with her friend Helen Connelly and her husband. Bill grimaced. How that nice woman had ever ended up with that man, Bill would never know.

'I wonder what crusade he'll be on tonight,' he muttered to himself.

Janice caught him before he left.

He had been right, she said. The victim had been a student. James Fenton. Studying Computer Science at Glasgow University. The people at the Computing Department recognised him from the photograph.

'They told the Constable he hadn't logged onto the system for the last few days, Sir. Apparently he was a frequent user before. Spent a lot of his time there.'

'Surprise, surprise! So, have we contacted the parents?'

'The mother, Sir. They're divorced. The boy lives, lived, with the mother when he was at home. We've contacted the Manchester force. Someone should be round there by now.'

'So we didn't need the birthmark after all?'

'Sorry, Sir?'

'Nothing, Janice.'

Now the boy was real. He had a name, an occupation, a home and a mother.

We'll have to bring the mother up, Bill thought, to identify the body. Some job that would be. What a world. And he still had a night of Jim Connelly to face.

When he got home, Margaret was already dressed for dinner. She glanced at the kitchen clock, then threw him a look that sent him straight to the shower. But she must have relented a little, because when he stepped out of the cubicle there was a glass of whisky deposited by the sink. He carried it through to the bedroom to find his clothes already laid out on the bed.

As he dressed, he could hear Margaret giving last minute orders to whichever of the kids was going to be around that night. He heard her voice and what closely resembled a moan following it. Whatever she was saying, someone didn't like it. She came in, just as he was finishing knotting his tie.

'Ready?'

He gave her a nod.

'Just as well. Jim and Helen will be here in a minute to pick us up.'

He pulled a face but she wasn't at the jollying stage yet.

'Just be glad you're not driving,' she said. 'At least you can take a drink and relax for a change.'

As he walked down the garden path, Bill wasn't surprised to see Helen Connelly behind the wheel. Jim Connelly wasn't a man to give up his drink, even on his wife's night out.

Helen smiled out at him, her face slightly concerned. 'We were worried you might have to call off at the last minute.'

'He knows better.' Margaret gave his arm a squeeze and Bill suddenly wished he was going out alone with his wife. It had been too long since they had sat talking over a meal together. He slid into the back seat beside her and took her hand and she smiled at him. He would make an effort for her sake.

'So, Bill. How's the murder investigation going?' Connelly turned round to look at him.

The man has been drinking already, Bill decided. His face was flushed, his voice too loud. Margaret had said Connelly was trying to cut down on the booze. Helen was getting worried by the quantity of work and drink her husband seemed addicted to. He doesn't know how lucky he is, thought Bill. Helen could have had her pick at university.

Helen smiled in the rear-view mirror at him and he felt mean. After all, hadn't Margaret said Helen and Jim were happy together? She and Helen had been friends since their student days. Then they had taught together in the same primary school for years, until Margaret left to have the kids. Helen never had any kids. Maybe that was the problem. Come to think of it, Connelly treated every newspaper story like his kid. His baby. The man just didn't know how to compromise. Much like himself.

'*You* tell *me* how it's going.' Bill laughed as if he meant it. 'We both know the *News* is always one step ahead of us.'

'True,' Connelly said with a grin. 'By the way, the guy who owns the flat you found the boy in? We found some stuff on him a couple of years back. We had no proof so we didn't use it.'

'Oh?' Bill tried to keep the interest out of his voice. One thing he had to say about Connelly, the man was hellish good at ferreting out information. He had been responsible for lifting the lid on a number of criminal activities in the past. Ever since their university days together, when Connelly had filled the student newspaper with tales of corrupt landlords and student grant scams, he had been able to sniff out a story. His methods were unconventional and irritating, but Bill had to admit, he had his uses.

'I'll send you the information over, if you like,' Connelly was saying, 'without the contact name of course.'

'Of course.'

Bill was not going to rise to the bait. He turned and smiled serenely at Margaret. If things didn't go well tonight, it wouldn't be his fault.

But Connelly wasn't finished yet.

'I'm working on a piece just now that might interest you.'

'Really?' Bill was almost certain the damned man licked his lips.

'All about Freemasons and the police force.'

Bill had difficulty controlling his voice. That was the last thing he wanted to hear about, even if the Super was one.

'No use talking to me about that, Jim. The Freemasons don't let Catholics in, lapsed or otherwise.'

Margaret nudged him in the ribs.

'Enough!' Helen was shouting in exasperation. 'Haven't you two got anything else to talk to one another about except work?'

No, thought Bill, that was the problem.

By the time they reached the Italian restaurant, Bill had already had enough of Jim Connelly. Tonight's topic was to be the Freemasons and their infiltration and corruption of the police force, whether he liked it or not.

But as things turned out, the food was good and the women, at least, talked sense. They were at the coffee stage when things began to deteriorate. Margaret and Helen disappeared to the Ladies and left Bill alone to defend the force again.

'So you see, Bill,' Connelly was saying seriously. Bill wondered if you could get thrown out of an Italian restaurant on Sauchiehall Street for hysteria.

'They're everywhere,' Connelly announced, looking about him. 'Got a finger in every pie.' He poked the table with his forefinger, then raised it and pointed at Bill. 'Including your little lot.'

Connelly finished his pronouncement with a wave at the waiter for another whisky. Bill had lost count of the journalist's intake. Bill was at least three behind him. Doubles at that. If Connelly was cutting down on the drink, it certainly wasn't tonight, he thought. And this boys together stuff just grated. He shook his head at the suggestion that he might like another whisky but Jim Connelly had gone past the point of listening to anyone except himself.

When the glasses arrived this time, there was a bottle with them.

'Tasted this one before?' Jim turned the bottle so Bill could read the label. 'Tomatin. The Big T. A twelve-year-old blend. Difficult to get. I acquired a few bottles from an acquaintance of mine. Maybe you know him. Judge MacKay?'

Bill shook his head at both the whisky and the name and wondered if Judge MacKay was a Freemason or whether he was just helping Jim Connelly with his enquiries.

'I think he was hoping I would keep my mouth shut about his Freemason connections,' Connelly said, tapping his nose.

Bill had his answer.

'You two ready to go?' Helen had appeared behind her husband. 'It's getting late.'

'Sure?' Bill stood up.

'Our treat. Eh, Helen?' Connelly said, his voice slurred.

Bill caught Helen's eye. She went over to the cash desk with him.

'Thanks,' she said.

'What for?'

'You know. Not losing the head at him. He can be a pain in the neck when he's involved in a story. Investigative journalism, he calls it.'

'I'm much the same myself. Ask Margaret.'

She smiled at him. 'This murder enquiry, have you found out who the boy was yet?'

'As a matter of fact we have. The mother will know by now, and the *News* too, I expect.'

'Jim'll go after this, you know.'

Bill smiled sympathetically at her, wondering how often Margaret had said the same thing about him.

The car was silent on the way back. Helen concentrated on the road. Margaret leaned against Bill, her eyes half closed. Connelly seemed lost in thought. When they reached the house, Bill thanked Helen for a good night, thinking Connelly was asleep. He wasn't. When they got out, he rolled down the passenger window and called after them as they went up the path.

'Judge MacKay is a good friend of Sir James Dalrymple, you know. And Sir James plays golf with your Superintendent . . . Cosy, isn't it?'

Bill lifted his hand in a wave, as the car took off. The trouble was, Connelly was probably right. Well, good luck to him. If he was brave enough to lift the lid on the upper echelons of the police force, he was a braver man than most.

8

CHRISSY MOVED FROM one foot to the other to kill the cramp. Apart from having cramp in one leg and wet feet, she was also pissed off. Neil had told her to wait here for him, he would only be five minutes. That had been fifteen minutes ago. Three cars had slowed down beside her and one had stopped and offered her twenty quid for a blow job. When she shook her head, the man upped his offer to twenty-five.

So, she thought, there was another job where you got to examine as much semen as you liked. And definitely better paid.

Chrissy pulled her jacket tighter across her chest and stuck her hands in her pockets. Late May or not, it was cold out here. She decided she would give him five more minutes then she was off. Easy money or not.

It hadn't been difficult to get access to records. Soliciting by rent boys was logged where police had cautioned or charged male prostitutes or their clients. When she read the list, she'd thanked God Patrick hadn't been cautioned as a client, yet. Then she saw the photo of Neil and realised who it was. The charge was dated the previous year, but she had convinced herself the address might still be valid. And it was.

When Neil appeared round the side of the building, he nodded at her to walk beside him and took off down a side street. The street lamps were coming on, glossy red against the grey night. Chrissy tried to keep up with him, but he was walking fast and she was always a step behind. His collar was up, his hands in his pockets too. It seemed this way of walking was compulsory round here.

It was funny seeing Neil MacGregor again. Chrissy hadn't seen him since she was at school, or since he last went to school. She had really fancied him rotten then, she remembered, though she hadn't let on. Not even to her best mate, Irene. Neil had been the bane of his form teacher's life. Poor Miss Smith had spent a lot of time trying to get him to come back to school, but she hadn't succeeded. Then he disappeared from home too.

'In here,' Neil said.

The main door was off its hinges, slammed back against the wall. There was dog dirt on the step and he pushed her out of the way of it and nodded to her to follow him up the stairs. The stair lights weren't working and Chrissy had to hold onto the banister and keep looking up, where faint street light seeped in through the cupola. His place was on the third floor and when he opened the door she was relieved to get inside.

The front door opened onto a small hall which led into a long room. Chrissy expected the room to be a mess and was surprised to find she was wrong. There was a double bed at one end. The wall nearest the door held a couch (sloping slightly), a chair, a telly and a stereo. It was better than the room she had at home.

He locked the door behind her and Chrissy had a sudden thought that she was stupid coming in here with him, alone. But when he turned to face her, he had that same old grin on his face, as full of cheek as ever.

'Funny,' he said. 'I always wanted to shag Chrissy McInsh. All the time we went to school together.'

'I was the only one you didn't shag.'

He laughed. It was true. Everybody, except Chrissy. Even Irene had succumbed in the end. She thought she could change Neil, just like Miss Smith. But she was wrong. No one could change Neil.

'Still as tight-arsed as ever?' he was asking.

'Aye.'

They both laughed and he nodded at her to sit down on the sloping couch. Then he went through to the kitchen that led off the living room and brought back two glasses and a bottle.

'Vodka?' he said.

'And orange?'

'Get fucked!'

'Not by you,' Chrissy said firmly.

Neil laughed again and pulled off his jacket. Chrissy saw the weals on his neck. His hand followed her eyes and he rubbed at the healing skin.

'Fucking old queer,' he said, sitting down beside her. Somewhere below them the left leg of the couch slid nearer the floor. 'Funny, eh?' he said. 'I used to be the one doing the shagging.' He threw back the glass and let the clear liquid slide down his throat.

Chrissy waited until he finished then said, 'I need to speak to you, about Patrick.'

Neil looked at her curiously. 'You mean your brother? The big one with the brains?'

Chrissy nodded.

Neil poured another shot.

'Lucky night,' he said, toasting her. 'Better than that Buckfast pish, anyway.'

He pulled out a cigarette packet and offered her one. She shook her head.

'Always were a good wee Fenian lassie.'

'You were an altar boy,' Chrissy reminded him.

'Aye.' Neil blew smoke at the ceiling. 'It was Father Riley that taught me all I needed to know in that wee back room of his.' He laughed again, bitterly this time, and looked at Chrissy to see if he had shocked her.

Chrissy hadn't been allowed in the back room of the chapel, with or without Father Rilcy. It seemed being a Catholic girl had had its blessings after all.

'Somebody's blackmailing Patrick,' she said.

'Why?'

'He's gay.'

'Fucking stupid word,' Neil said. 'None of the ones I meet are any fun. So what do you want me to do?'

'I want to know who it is.'

'And you think I can find out?'

Neil looked at her shrewdly.

'Got any money?' he asked.

She took out the hundred she'd taken from the cashpoint.

'It's not a crime to be gay, you know.'

She gave him a look that said it all.

'Oh, I see, once a Catholic always a Catholic.'

'I don't care about all that. It's his job at the school.
If the Marist brothers find out about this, he'll have to
leave. And my dad and my brothers . . . they hate that
sort of thing. If my dad finds out Patrick's gay, he'll
ban him from the house and my mum won't get to see
him.'

'Happy families, eh? Did you bring the note?'

She handed it over.

'Patrick hasn't seen it,' she said. 'It came to the house
and my mother opened it. I told her it was just somebody jealous of Patrick.'

He whistled. 'Your big brother's running with the
wrong people, Chrissy. He wants to get a nice steady
boyfriend.'

'Don't.'

'Okay. If I get you a name, what are you going to do
then?'

She shook her head because she didn't know. All she
wanted at the moment was a name. That was enough.

Neil looked at his watch.

'I've got to go now.'

Chrissy handed him the lab phone number.

'I know where you work,' Neil said, stuffing the bit of
paper in his pocket. 'I've seen you from the park.'

When Chrissy reached the street, it had started to
spit. A big car was parked along the road under a street
lamp, its soft velvet grey touched with drops of rain.
When she reached the corner she turned to see Neil
open the back door of the car and slip inside.

★   ★   ★

Neil MacGregor had lived along the road from Chrissy until his father finally chucked him out of the house for good. His father was a wide boy himself and there wasn't room for two wide boys in the same house. Mrs MacGregor had enough on her hands looking after one.

Neil's father liked a wee drink. A wee drink taken frequently and especially on a Thursday night when half the population of the street was in the pub while the other half were at the bingo; or in Chrissy's mother's case at something in the chapel.

If ever a man was prayed for, Chrissy thought, it was her father.

Chrissy's mother called Neil a wee toe-rag, but there was something about him that would 'get him a jeely piece at any door'.

When Neil's big brother joined the parachute regiment and was sent to Belfast, Neil's mother and Chrissy's mother had their own line of candles in the chapel for him. It didn't stop him being killed, his stomach blown out and splattered on a woman with a pram who was walking by. Neil's father liked a wee drink even more after that, and Mrs MacGregor lost sight of Neil in her endless trips to the chapel.

Chrissy laid her face against the bus window and watched the drops of rain skid off in annoyance. Neil hadn't changed much. The dark hair and blue eyes (shanty Irish, her mother used to call him), and the grin that, in another city, might have made him a movie star.

The bus began to crawl up through St George's
Cross and onto Maryhill Road. On the right, a block of
flats loomed out of the rain.

Chrissy and Patrick had been two of the few on her
street 'to make good', outside the ones that joined the
army. Chrissy's three other brothers existed on hand-
outs from her, Patrick and the State. Sometimes she
thought they were the lucky ones. If she hadn't been
giving away so much of her wages she could have
moved into a flat of her own and she would have been
headed there now instead of sitting on the bus back to
Maryhill.

If there was one thing she'd learned in chapel, it was
to suffer in silence. Father Riley had taught the weans
that well. Even Neil had kept his mouth shut. Old Riley
was gone now. Not to a better place, but to an old folks'
home for retired priests. Not much chance of a wee
fuck in the back room there.

When the bus stopped at the terminus, Chrissy sat
until everyone else got out. She didn't want to walk
along with anyone and have to talk. She needed time
to rehearse her speech to her mother about how the
letter about Patrick was all bullshit (she'd have to find
another word for that because she wasn't allowed to
swear, even in a house that had heard the word 'fuck'
more often than the Pope said his prayers). Patrick
was seeing a girl, that's what she would tell her
mother. She'd met her, and he was even talking about
bringing her up to the house soon. Her name was
Teresa, so she must be one of us. If Chrissy got it
right her mother could miss her candle-lighting trip

tonight and might even sit down with a wee sherry and watch the telly.

Convincing her brothers, Chrissy knew, would be another matter.

9

SEAN WAS GONE. All that remained was the clatter of his feet on the stairs, the bang of the outside door and the retreating hum of the taxi. Rhona stood silently in a room that still echoed with his anger.

'This is stupid, Rhona. First you're not going, then you're going, then you're not going. What the fuck is going on?'

'I don't want to go, that's all.' She knew she sounded unreasonable.

'But you told Chrissy you were going. You took time off to go.'

'I've changed my mind.'

'Why?'

She didn't answer. Couldn't answer.

'If it's about the woman in the Art Gallery . . .'

She didn't want to talk about her so she interrupted. 'I can't leave the lab. We haven't finished the murder tests yet.'

'Fuck the murder tests.' He came towards her.

'Don't!'

'Don't what, Rhona?'

'Don't touch me!'

He stopped in his tracks and the look he gave her

froze her chest. She hadn't meant to say it like that. She didn't want him to touch her because it would make her go with him and she couldn't go and she couldn't tell him why.

She had never seen him angry before. He turned from her and headed for the door.

His voice was cold, remote. 'I'll phone you when I know where I'm staying.'

She had nodded, unable to argue any more. Now she felt suddenly bereft. She didn't want him to go like that, didn't want him to go at all. She wanted him here. She wanted to tell him what was really wrong. Tell him about this nightmare. Let him talk sense into her. But that would mean revealing herself. And she couldn't do that. Not now. Perhaps not ever.

As usual, everything important has been left unsaid, she told herself. She had simply created more ghosts between them.

Sean hadn't believed her excuses about the tests. He knew she was lying. They weren't short-staffed any more, either. Tony was back from his holiday in Mexico. In fact it was something Tony said that had given her the idea, that she might pretend to go to Paris with Sean.

'I agree with Chrissy,' he'd told her. 'You look like shit.'

'Thanks, Tony.'

'You need a break. Go with lover-boy to Paris, have endless sex and leave me to run this lab the way I want. For a week at least.'

So she'd agreed. She told Chrissy she would go. She

even went out with her after work on Thursday to buy new underwear for the trip.

But it was all a lie.

She had lied to Sean, made him think she was going. Until the last minute. The cruelty of her actions frightened her. She made excuses, saying to herself, if he could see another woman on the quiet, she could keep the truth from him.

Rhona switched on the gas fire, sat down on the couch, picked up a cushion and hugged it to her. The cat jumped up lightly and rubbed itself against the cushion, manoeuvring it into shape before it plopped down on top. Rhona stroked the velvety ears and the purring settled into a pleasant drone that began to calm her. If she had tried to tell Sean about the nightmares, she thought, she would have had to explain why the boy's death haunted her. He had been with her long enough to know that dealing with death was not normally a problem for her. She would have had to tell him about Liam. And she had never told anyone about Liam.

She had phoned the number the hospital gave her. A woman had answered. Sensing her reluctance to speak and the likelihood that the phone would be put down, the woman suggested calling in to talk things over with a counsellor. Rhona had made an appointment.

When the time came, she'd managed to find a million reasons why she couldn't go. Instead, she waited for an evening when Sean was playing at the jazz club, and phoned Edward at home. She explained about the murder and the birthmark and told him she had to know what had happened to their son.

The silence at the other end had been as deep as the chasm between them. Edward cleared his throat. He didn't think that would be wise but, and here he interrupted her angry reply, if she insisted on this line of action, there was someone he knew who might help. Rhona must agree to say nothing about any of this to anyone, not even her Irishman.

And she had agreed.

'I'll phone you back,' Edward said.

'When?'

'I don't know. Some time this week. And Rhona? If you're not in, I'm not leaving a message about this on an ansaphone.'

'You won't need to. I'll be here.'

So she told Chrissy and Tony she was taking the week off to go to Paris with Sean and she told Sean she couldn't go with him because she was too busy at work.

Rhona moved the protesting cat from her stomach and reached for the remote. She switched the television on, flicking through channels until she found the early evening news. She sat impatiently through the usual political headlines, then at last the announcer stated that there would now follow an appeal by the mother of the Glasgow murder victim. Flanked by two detectives, faced with a room full of journalists, sat a small, dark-haired woman. A woman who looked nothing like the murdered boy.

Rhona leaned back on the couch while the camera moved in, as if it needed to be closer to hear her whispered words, so close that Rhona could see the red swollen eyes, the skin sagging with distress. The

woman became suddenly aware of the camera and
drew herself up, taking a deep breath, and began.

My son has been murdered. Her voice pierced Rhona's heart. *He has been murdered by a madman. A
madman who preys on boys. My son was a clever boy.
A boy with a future. I loved him. Please help the police find
Jamie's killer. If you have children you will understand.*
Her voice began to falter. *Please, please tell the police
anything that might help, before this madman kills
again* . . . The words petered out and the camera
moved aside, as if embarrassed by so much grief.

Now it was the turn of the policeman on her right.

Bill looked exhausted but he was as professional
and cogent as ever. He evenly explained that the
murder victim, James Fenton, was a student of
Computing Science at Glasgow University. A quiet
hard working student, who kept himself to himself.
The police had in their possession a curtain that had
been spread beneath his body. It was their belief that
the murderer had left in a hurry and that he would
otherwise have taken this curtain with him. Someone
might recognise it.

The camera swung to the left. After the greyness of
grief, the bright swirling colours of the curtain dazzled
Rhona's eyes.

Rhona spent the next day sifting through forensic
journals for articles she had promised herself to read.
She went out briefly for fresh milk and bread and
hurried back, worried that Edward might phone in her
absence. But it was Sean who called first. He always

sounded more Irish on the phone, as if distance marked out who he was more clearly.

There was an awkward silence, then he told her he would be staying on for a second week.

'Why?' she asked, her voice small.

'The guy I'm filling in for has met a rich divorcee in Florida.' He was trying to joke to cover the awkwardness. 'He doesn't want to leave yet. So,' he said, and she could hear the caution in his voice, 'you could come out the second week.'

'Sean . . .'

'I'm sleeping on someone's couch at the moment but I can get us a hotel room. I'm off during the day. Springtime in Paris and all that.' He was waiting for an answer.

'I'm not sure.'

'I see.'

'I mean I'll need to check with work.'

Silence.

He gave her a number.

'You can try my mobile or this number.'

'Is that where you're staying?'

'No, it's the club.'

'Right.'

The call ended as badly as it began. As she hung up, the thought crossed her mind that Sean was not used to being turned down.

After tea she put on a video and sat down with a glass of wine. The cat resumed its favourite perch on her lap. Edward's call came at nine o'clock.

'There will be an envelope in tomorrow's post,' he

said. 'As you'll see, the murdered boy has nothing to do with you.'

'With us,' she corrected him.

He ignored that. 'I hope this is the end of the business.'

Rhona hung up without answering.

Of course, Edward would prefer to deal with this by letter. Speaking directly he might have to use Liam's name, or worse, refer to him as your child. Edward would never do that. Edward had always distanced himself from the event like a bad smell. And so it was. A bad smell come back to haunt him.

Rhona swallowed the remains of her wine and poured another glass. The cat grunted with displeasure and jumped off her tense body, opting for the more reliable comfort of the hearthrug instead.

Outside, the sky had cleared. Evening sun shone in. The room looked empty. Like my life, she thought.

Strange to look back and see emptiness where once she had seen success. Getting her degree. Studying for a PhD. The freedom to choose where she wanted to work. The delight in being given the responsibility for her own lab. Buying the flat. Money in the bank. Nothing. I have just been putting in time, she thought . . . until now.

The phone rang again. Rhona cursed herself for not switching on the ansaphone. Then it struck her that it might be Edward, calling back with something he'd forgotten to tell her. Something important.

'Is that Dr Rhona MacLeod?'

It was a man's voice.

'Yes?'

'This is going to sound really silly.' The man hesitated, then cleared his throat nervously. 'We met yesterday in the rain. My name's Gavin MacLean.'

'We shared a taxi.'

'I wonder whether you would like to come out with me tomorrow night to see a film,' he went on, before she could answer. 'I quite understand if you think I'm a nut and say no.'

'No.'

'Right.' He sounded disappointed.

'I mean I don't think you're a nut.' Rhona laughed.

'That's a relief. So you'll come?'

'I don't know.'

'A film. No strings.'

She thought about it. She would have the letter tomorrow. She didn't need to stay in any more. She needed to be normal again. He seemed nice. It was just a film. And if Sean could do it, why couldn't she?

'Okay. Just a film.'

'Great. I'll pick you up about eight?'

It wasn't until after Rhona had spent half an hour convincing herself that it was okay to go out with a strange man that she suddenly began to wonder how Gavin MacLean knew both her name and her home number.

10

THE NIGHT RHONA contacted him about the baby had
begun well for Edward. He and Fiona were holding a
dinner party with Sir James Dalrymple among the
guests. Edward knew he could count on Fiona's support.
She understood the importance of playing the game.

He had stood at the door and surveyed his sitting
room. June sunlight shone in through the French
windows and danced across the deep blues and pinks
of the Chinese rug, the chintz covered sofas and the
polished mahogany furniture. This room symbolised
everything he had worked for, from the silk-framed
windows overlooking the trim lawn, to the flower vases
(expensive vases, expensive flowers), and the well-
stocked drinks cabinet.

Without Fiona, her contacts and her family, he
might never have got this far. He was good at his
job, but there were many others who were just as good.
Fiona had made the difference.

Through the open double doors to the dining room
he could see her, still in her dressing gown, putting the
last touches to an already perfect table. As she bent to
rearrange the centre-piece, Edward admired both his
wife's attention to detail and her exposed thigh.

Edward had already poured Fiona two whiskies, ostensibly with plenty of water, but in reality rather strong, being hopeful that some time between arranging the table centre and the donning of her little black number, she would let him make love to her.

Fiona was looking over at him, wanting him to give the table arrangement his final approval. Edward gave her the response she was looking for. Then he inclined his head towards the stairs and their bedroom above. Fiona smiled.

Edward had met Fiona at a drinks party held by his firm and a corporate client, in the client's luxury offices overlooking the Clyde. He was feeling pleased with himself that evening, having completed an overseas transaction that had saved this particular client a fortune in UK tax. And the truth was, he was glad to be out of the apartment. The situation between himself and Rhona had hit rock bottom.

Fiona looked so good in black. It was something about the combination of upmarket blondeness and lightly tanned skin. That particular evening the black dress was cut to show the outline of Fiona's buttocks.

Rhona and he had not had sex in a long time. Edward suddenly felt like a teenager with his first erection.

Halfway through the evening, Fiona had invited him up to her office, two floors above the party.

Edward had leaned Fiona against the imposing mahogany desk and slipped down the thin straps of her dress, exposing her pert breasts.

Fiona released herself from his mouth to slide down and rest her face in his crotch and Edward had a terrible desire to let his prick erupt there and then.

But Fiona's timing had been perfect.

She had turned from him and bent over the table and Edward had his wish. Across the leather-topped desk he opened Fiona's tight little buttocks and slid inside. And if the party below didn't hear his cries of delight, it meant they had the eminently suitable music turned up much too loud.

Even now, all these years later, Fiona had the same effect on him. There had been other women since then, as he knew there had been men with Fiona. But they had stayed together. They both knew they were stronger together than apart.

The hum of conversation around the dining table confirmed the success of Fiona's seating plan. There were eight guests, all involved in one way or another with the by-election campaign. Opposite Edward, Fiona was deep in conversation with Judge Cameron MacKay. Fiona had already told Edward that the 65-year-old had difficulty locating his own knee at times and his hand was often to be found stroking the female thigh next to him, which tonight was Fiona's.

Edward had already dropped his napkin in order to see just how energetic Judge MacKay's hand was. What he saw made him marvel at his wife's calm demeanour.

The rest of the group was made up of two business clients (Party supporters) and a number of activists, the most attractive of whom was Sarah Anderson. Sarah, Edward had decided, was a dyke, since she had never given him the slightest indication she found him attractive. Still, he thought, looking appreciatively across the table at her, even dykes have breasts and there was something rather enticing about the shape of hers.

On the left of Sarah sat Ian Urquhart, Edward's campaign manager. Ian wasn't interested in Sarah. His inclinations lay elsewhere. Tonight Fiona had placed him beside Sir James Dalrymple.

And, thought Edward, it looked as if Fiona had been right about Sir James after all.

When the phone rang, the party had been about to adjourn to the conservatory for a nightcap. Fiona gave Edward a nod and went to answer it, annoyed, he could tell, that Amy hadn't got there already. By the time she came back, Edward had ushered their guests into the conservatory and settled them with their drinks. It was just as well, or they would have seen Fiona's face.

'It's a woman,' she said coldly. 'She wants to speak to you.'

Edward used one of his 'probably a constituent' sort of smiles, but Fiona wasn't convinced that easily.

'You're not an MP yet,' she reminded him as she swept past and into the conservatory.

As soon as Rhona spoke Edward knew she had been crying. It struck him as strange that after all these years something inside him hurt because of that. She was rambling on about a birthmark and a dead boy.

When she paused for breath, Edward found himself promising to find out what she wanted to know. Anything to shut her up and get her out of his face. He said goodbye and lifted the whisky glass from where he had laid it a few minutes before, when life was sweet. His hand was actually trembling. The jolt of straight whisky failed to dissolve the dread that gripped him. Edward made an effort to organise his thoughts, trying to get things into perspective. Rhona had always been neurotic, especially after the baby was born. Fiona had never been like that. Fiona had taken birth in her stride. Had been out playing tennis a few days later. But not Rhona. Months of coldness and rejection. It had been torture. Edward flinched at the memory. Thank God he had moved on. And now the scene in the Art Gallery – all he'd done was make a simple request. He should never have gone near her. It had been a mistake. Now of all times!

Edward downed his whisky and returned to the dining room to refill it from the decanter. Then he took a deep breath and walked back into the conservatory.

He nodded serenely at his wife and sat down next to Sarah Anderson, who for once gave him a welcoming smile. He smiled back, making a mental note that certain priorities must be addressed: nothing (not babies, dead boys, or even seduction) must stand in the way of the conversation he meant to have with Sir James Dalrymple tonight.

II

THE BEDROOM WAS untidy. There were discarded tee-
shirts on the floor and three empty glasses on the
bedside table, sticky with Diet Coke. His sock drawer
sat open and there was the smell of old cigarette ash.
He'd been hiding the fag ends in the drawer along with
his socks. Now there were too many of them in the box
and every time he opened the drawer to get clean socks,
Jonathan could smell them. Since his mother had
'handed over his room to him', as she put it, it had
got easier to hide evidence of his smoking. Now Amy,
their housekeeper, didn't bring the clean washing into
the room any more. Instead she left it in a pile on the
floor outside the door. Since she'd stopped coming in
he didn't need to dispose of the fag ends one at a time.
But now if he put them in the kitchen bin, Amy would
notice the smell and tell his mother.

Jonathan took a last drag, stubbed the cigarette out
on the ledge and closed the window, adding the dog
end to the overflowing box. Thinking about what he
would do with them was about all he could manage at
the moment.

He went over to his wardrobe and rummaged about
at the back. Below him the party had moved into the

conservatory. He'd heard the dining room chairs being scraped across the parquet floor and the rumble of conversation as they all moved out. Then the phone rang and Jonathan hoped for a brief moment it might be Mark. A glance at the clock told him Mark would be out and about by this time. Phoning Jonathan would be the last thing on his mind. You wouldn't catch Mark staying in on a Saturday night.

The hall was directly below Jonathan's bedroom, so he always knew when someone was coming up the stairs. It also meant he could listen in to phone calls. Tonight he could tell his father was pissed off with the caller from his clipped tone.

Jonathan found the vodka bottle stashed in a boot at the back of the wardrobe and pulled it out. He had agreed, when they acquired it from the drinks cabinet, to share it with his sister Morag. But despite being only ten months older than him, she seemed to be able to get drink when she was out. Jonathan walked over to the three glasses, selected the least sticky one and poured himself a shot. The fresh orange he'd mixed it with didn't smell too good and he wondered whether it had gone off.

The lights from the conservatory lit up the garden. If he stood very close to his window and pressed his face against the glass, he could make out the two seats closest to the French windows that opened onto the lawn. The young woman he'd let in earlier was there. Jonathan squirmed, remembering how friendly she had been when he'd opened the door to her and how, once he'd noticed she had no bra on, he'd been too embarrassed to answer any of her questions.

Now her attention was directed towards his father, who had on his special 'attractive woman' face. Jonathan took a slug of the vodka, relishing the blast as it slid down. Then he put down the glass and unzipped his jeans and took out his thing. It lay there flopped to one side, pale and blue veined against the denim. He reached down and touched it with the cold glass and it jumped away from him. Outside the girl was standing up now, her face turned towards the house, the light green gauze material of her dress folding about her breasts. He stared at her, imagining what her tits looked like under that dress, while he rubbed the cold glass up and down his prick.

It was always better to wait until his parents were asleep before logging on. Usually he had to put up with Morag coming home and telling him things she had or hadn't done that night, but she was in already. She'd come home about midnight and gone straight to her room, so he didn't have to suffer a blow by blow account of her night's exploits. After that he usually had to sit through all the snorting and panting from his parents' room. Ever since his father had been offered the candidacy he'd been poking away merrily. Jonathan wondered how his mother put up with the smarmy bastard. At least he wouldn't have to sit through that noise tonight. His parents had been at it earlier. He'd heard them when he came up to his room.

Now the house was asleep, the only hum of life coming from the pale blue computer screen in the corner.

Jonathan's first thought was to send Mark an email. Something that would make him laugh, something about his parents having it off before the dinner party. Mark usually checked his emails when he came in, however late it was.

Jonathan clicked on the icon and waited.

There were two emails waiting for him.

When Jonathan first realised that his father was a wanker it had come as a shock. When he was small Edward hadn't been around much. His mother always said he was working. And when he did come home, he was tired. So Morag and he went to their mother for what they needed, or more often to Amy, who had worked in the house for as long as Jonathan could remember. Amy was a pal but she had strict ideas of right and wrong. Drinking and smoking and sex 'at his age' were wrong, and Jonathan had never built up enough courage to ask her when they became right. When he was small, he stayed with Amy while his mother was 'out'. Where 'out' was, Jonathan never knew, but his mother always smelled nice when she went there. It wasn't work, he knew that, but when she came home she was 'exhausted' and would collapse on the sofa and ask him to bring her the drink she'd taught him to make. One thing he did know was that his family was respectable, well off, and Tory. They didn't like blacks, browns (except tans gained on foreign holidays), yellows, or lefties. They thought you should stand on your own two feet (even if you only had one), and that a move to London was going up in the world.

When Jonathan was about ten he'd been brought home by a friend's mother earlier than expected. The car dropped him at the big gate and when he saw his father's car sitting outside the house, he suddenly didn't want to go in and be questioned (they called it having a conversation), so he'd decided to go and check out his SSTD (special secret tree den) before he went in the kitchen to look for Amy. He'd slipped across the front lawn and round the side of the house into the orchard, then ran through the thickness of apple blossom, darting this way and that as if he was being followed. He slid through the door in the garden wall, with one last glance to convince himself that the enemy hadn't seen his escape. Already he could hear the sound of the river and the trees were crowding in on him with rustling voices. Jonathan loved the wood. It wasn't like the front of the house, with its flowering rhododendrons dotting the anorexic lawn. Here things grew just the way they wanted. Big and bold, heavy and sweet. Jonathan could smell them growing, especially when he lay down in his den, his face close to the earth.

He had walked quickly, anxious to get to his den. The ancient pine tree that marked its location was twisted with years, its trunk split in two, to form younger branches. On three sides of it huddled gorse and juniper and patches of thorny brambles. On the fourth side, the path opened up into a patch of grass and sunlight. Jonathan circled the tree until he was out of sight of the path, then threw himself on the ground and slid along on his belly, avoiding the sharp thorns of the brambles. The ground began to dip below him and he rolled down into his den with a grunt of delight.

He was lying there looking up at the thick canopy of foliage that was his roof, when he heard voices. He sat up a little, enough to peer out through his special peephole at the couple who walked towards him along the path. The woman was young and pretty. She wore a bright blue dress lit up by the sunlight that dropped down through the rustling leaves. She laughed, a tinkling sound that made the hairs on the back of Jonathan's neck stand up.

Then he heard the man's voice. It was his father.

Jonathan pressed himself to the ground, his heart thumping so hard that he knew they must hear it. But they had no ears or eyes for anything but themselves. When the talking and laughing stopped, there was something in the sudden silence that made Jonathan squirm against the earth floor, twisting round to get a better view. The woman was backed against the tree so that he could only see a line of leg on either side. There was a frantic scrabbling sound and then one of her legs was up and round his father and the other was in mid air, swaying wildly with each pumping motion. Now all he could hear was the squeak and moan of her voice.

Pump pump pump pump and then her shoe began to loosen, swinging on her toes for a moment before it dropped onto the grass.

When Jonathan got back to the house, after waiting a full half hour by the watch his father had given him for Christmas, Edward was at the front door, busy telling Fiona that he had arrived home minutes before her.

From then on Jonathan knew everything his father said was a lie.

The first email was from Mark. He must have sent it before he went out because it said, *Yo! I've just put on the pulling juice and I'm off. Think of Shona Seaton's tits and you'll know where I am.*

Jonathan tried to think of a reply that would make Mark laugh. But anything he said would be made up, and talking about your parents having sex rather than you having sex was sad. He wondered why Mark bothered emailing him. At school Mark was usually too busy being cool to be seen with him.

Jonathan went for the vodka and this time drank it straight from the bottle. It was having the desired effect. He supposed he could tell Mark about the cold glass wank and the tits in the conservatory. It would be better than nothing. But he didn't click on Reply. Instead he had another drink, knowing he was putting off the moment when he would open the second email.

It had been going on for three months now. The first message had come apparently by accident. Jonathan had spent a week setting up his own homepage, putting in some of his likes and dislikes. It had been meant for a competition in a PC magazine but after he designed it he suddenly didn't want to enter it after all. After it was uploaded, his homepage had brought half a dozen replies. Four liked the same football team as Jonathan and two told him to fuck off and get a life by supporting another one. Then things went quiet until the first message from Simon.

Jonathan had spent a lot of time talking to Simon after that first message. It had been exam time and his father had been moaning on about Law again and what grades he'd have to get if he was going to do Law at Edinburgh or fucking Cambridge. Who wanted to go to fucking Cambridge? Who wanted to do fucking Law anyway, Jonathan said, and Simon had agreed. You should study what you really like, Simon said, and if that was Art then that was what you should do. Simon even sent him information on various Art colleges and web addresses where he could find out more.

Jonathan never really thought about Simon's age. Electronically, age didn't matter. It was obvious they thought alike. One night he'd moaned on about girls. Simon had talked to him for a long time after that, and a lot of what he said about girls was true.

He laid down the bottle and tried to open the drawer of his desk. The handle was a little hazy and kept moving when he reached for it but eventually he caught it and pulled it open. He had put the first pictures he'd printed out in there under his school books. They were inside an old Algebra jotter. His mother would never look in that.

The ink cartridge on the printer had been running out and the printouts were faded in parts but you could still see what they were doing in them. Jonathan riffled through until he found his favourite.

He scrabbled about with his zipper but either the drink, the bad orange or the earlier pull had rendered his thing unconscious so he had another drink instead.

When the second lot of printouts arrived he'd looked

at them, then torn them up. The third set he'd looked at for a lot longer, then taken them and hidden them at the SSTD. He hadn't been down there for over a week now and he had pretty much made up his mind to burn them. He stuffed the pictures in the drawer and looked at the screen. The unread email was big, which probably meant it contained graphics.

Jonathan finished the vodka, double-clicked on the screen and opened it.

12

THE ENVELOPE ARRIVED by the first post.

Rhona was already awake. The rattle of the letter-box made her heart jump into her throat. She got up and hurried through to the hall. A large brown envelope lay on the carpet. She picked it up, carried it through to the kitchen and laid it on the table. Then she put the kettle on. She had waited seventeen years, she could wait a few minutes more.

Her parents had never known about their grandson. Right to the end, Rhona kept it from them. After her dad retired they had moved out of the city, back to the west coast where he was born. Rhona had spent her childhood holidays there, running along the shore, climbing the rocks he told her were the oldest in the world. As a student, Rhona had visited often, stealing long weekends from her studies, or a week in the summer. She loved the house with its white face staring out to sea. Being there was like being a child again, going fishing, walking the shoreline. She had taken Edward with her once. He had sat in the kitchen nursing a dram, talking to her parents. She had loved him then. But when they left, chugging along the road in their rebuilt MG, he had told her how he didn't like the wilds, that he was a city boy. She never took him back. When she found out she was pregnant and they decided to have the baby adopted, she couldn't face her parents and she made excuses when her mother phoned; pressure of work, she would see them in the summer when it was all over.

The baby would have been five when her mother died. Rhona started going home at weekends to see her father and each time she returned there was less of him. Once or twice he came to Glasgow to stay with her and they went back to the Gallery, but now the bottom level was all he could manage. As they retraced their familiar routes, she watched his face light up and she knew she had cheated him of something very precious.

Edward and she lasted six months after the adoption. That was all they could stand. Love and hate. Hate and love. She hated him for persuading her (did he?), and hated herself even more for being persuaded. And Edward? He just hated the messiness of it all.

The address on the envelope was in Edward's handwriting. This was one job he hadn't got his secretary to do. Rhona stared at it for a long time, then carefully slit it open, her mouth dry.

She pulled out two sheets of paper. The top one was a copy of a birth certificate. Her hands shook as she read the words. *Liam James MacLeod, born 2.35am Monday 2nd January, 1985*. She had never seen the birth certificate before. Edward had registered the birth. No use brooding, he'd said, it'll be easier if I do it and then you can put it all out of your mind. We have to get on with our lives. Rhona touched the writing. In the mother's box was her own name, Rhona Elizabeth MacLeod. The father's box was empty. Edward had said it was better that way.

'Then I can't come back when he's a millionaire and ask him for money,' he'd said with a laugh.

The second sheet was a short sharp note.

'I enclose a copy of the birth certificate. As you know, a birth parent has no statutory rights to trace events or gain access to Court papers. However, I have found out that the adoption was processed a month after the birth. Contact was then made with the registrars and an adoptive certificate issued in the name of Hope. A friend of mine in the police force tells me that the dead rent boy has been identified as a James Fenton from Manchester.'

Of course there was no connection between the two boys. Edward was right. She had been imagining things. Liam was out there, alive and happy. Edward had tidied up her life for her. Again.

By the time Gavin MacLean arrived at eight o'clock, Rhona had already drunk two gins. One while she sat in the bath and cried, the other as she got dressed, dried her hair and repaired her face.

When the buzzer went, she looked out of the window. Gavin was standing on the pavement. He waved when he spotted her and she waved back. When she emerged at street level, they both stood awkwardly for a moment.

'This is a bit embarrassing,' he said.

'Yes, it is.'

He was even taller than she'd thought, his hair blonder now that it was no longer wet, but his eyes and smile were the same.

'You look nice,' he said.

'I'm not as wet as last time.'

They both smiled. 'I thought if we ate first, it would break the ice.' He looked faintly nervous. 'So I booked an Italian.'

'Fine.'

She decided as they walked along together that she would offer to pay half. Keep things even between them.

'You can pay half,' he said, reading her mind, 'if it makes you feel more comfortable.'

As they crossed the road, he took her arm to guide her through the traffic. It suddenly reminded Rhona of crossing the road with her dad.

Rhona looked at Gavin blankly. Whatever he had said demanded an answer and she hadn't a clue what to say, because she hadn't been listening to him for the last five minutes.

'Sorry.'

'It's okay.'

He poured her some more wine and she lifted her glass and sipped it, avoiding his eyes.

'I have . . . there's something on my mind,' she apologised.

'Work?'

'Yes,' she said. It seemed easier.

'Want to talk about it?'

'I don't want to depress you.'

'You won't.'

'Well,' she began. 'I've been working on a case recently . . . a boy found murdered in a flat.'

'The student?'

'Yes.' She looked up, puzzled. 'How did you know?'

'I read the papers, *and* watch television.'

'Of course.' She felt silly. The whole of Scotland knew about the murdered boy. 'It's just,' she paused, 'this one got to me a bit. He looked like someone I know. That's all.'

'I see. Shall we skip the film?' he said.

'Please.'

He waved the waiter over and asked for the bill.

'Look. Why don't we go back to my place, listen to some music . . .'

'I don't want you to think . . .'

'I don't.'

Back in his comfortable flat drinking coffee, Rhona told him that she should be in Paris with Sean. She didn't say why she hadn't gone and he didn't ask. Instead he told her a bit about himself. He was forty, not married but had lived with someone for a long time, seven years in fact.

'I kept asking her to marry me and she kept saying no,' he explained, pulling a face. 'She had this thing about marriage. Her father was in the Merchant Navy so he only came home every six months. Her mother brought up the three of them on her own. When her father came back, he "wanted his place", as she put it, and her mother agreed. The kids didn't. Eventually her younger brother had a stand up fight with him in the house. She always said she would never marry.'

'So why did you break up?'

He hesitated as if searching for a reason. 'We got to this place where the road sort of ended. She got an offer of a job down south. We said we'd keep in touch but we didn't.'

'I think women and men are incompatible,' Rhona said. 'Different agendas.'

'Don't say that.'

'It's true. Maybe being gay is the answer.'

'Maybe it is.'

They looked at one another and laughed.

'I have to go,' she said.

'Right. I'll phone for a taxi.'

He went with her to the front door. Outside the air had turned warm. Scotland had at last remembered it was June.

'I never asked you how you got my home number?' she said.

Gavin looked embarrassed. 'I hacked it,' he admitted. 'Everyone's on a file somewhere. I can find out just about anything I want to know about a person from a computer, just like you can from their bodily fluids.'

'*1984* and all that?'

'That's right.'

The taxi drew up.

'Can I hack in again some time?' he asked.

'Only if I can test your bodily fluids.' She realised what she'd said after the words were out.

He laughed and raised his eyebrows. 'Any time.'

When Rhona got back to her flat, the green message light was flashing on the ansaphone. She pressed the play button. It was Sean. There was background music and halfway through his message, a high-pitched giggle, then a girl saying 'Sean' in a pleading voice. He said he would try again tomorrow night and reminded her of the club number. Rhona wondered why he hadn't given her the number of the flat where he was staying. Maybe he was staying with the giggly girl.

The second message was from Edward, hoping she had received the envelope.

'I sincerely hope, Rhona, that this will be the end of the matter.'

Rhona said shit very loudly. She went through to the bedroom, opened the envelope and took out the two papers and looked at them again. If Gavin MacLean could find out all about her by hacking, maybe he could find out more about her son.

And, she decided, Edward Stewart could get fucked.

13

BILL WILSON HAD had a sleepless night. Twice he'd gone downstairs and sat watching a late night movie until he'd started to drop off. But as soon as he got back into bed, he was wide awake again. Once light began to peek through the slit in the curtains, he gave up and got up for good. On automatic, he made himself coffee and sat down at the kitchen table.

Halfway through his second cup he heard someone walk along the upstairs landing to the toilet. It wasn't Margaret's step. He'd left her sound asleep. Twenty years living with a policeman had trained her to ignore his nocturnal habits.

A bedroom door clicked shut and then there was a series of taps and a long thin cackling whine and he realised that one of the kids was logging on to the Internet.

If all the kids were doing that, he thought, playing with the Internet while their parents were asleep, it would be hellish easy to access whatever they liked. He stood up and then sat down again. He'd already talked to them both about it.

Jamie Fenton had by all accounts been a good student up until two weeks before his death. He'd been staying in a new hall of residence, Dalrymple Hall, built with a little help from the generous Sir James Dalrymple. Paedophiles could get at vulnerable kids through the Internet, but the Computing Department at Glasgow assured him that the labs were supervised to ensure no 'dodgy surfing', as they called it.

Mrs Fenton had told him Jamie couldn't afford to buy a computer. He was on a grant and a student loan and she couldn't give him anything herself.

When Bill brought up the subject of sex, Mrs Fenton became agitated. Her son was normal, she protested. He had a girlfriend in Manchester, a nice girl that he went out with when he was home.

They'd got no leads from his fellow students, either. Jamie was a loner and spent most of his spare time in the computer lab. He was constantly broke. He'd been trying to borrow money to see himself through to the end of the session. It was tough being a student now, tougher than in his day, Bill realised.

He stood up and rinsed his cup at the sink. The early morning sun reminded him of his promise to Margaret to cut the grass. The paper boy skidded to a halt on his bicycle and came whistling up the path. Bill picked up the paper from the hall floor and spread it out on the kitchen table. The last thing he expected was to see his investigation blown wide open.

Helen Connelly answered the phone.

'Helen? It's Bill Wilson. Sorry to phone you this early. Is Jim about?'

'He's still in bed, Bill. He wasn't in till late. Something special came in last night. They held this morning's edition for it.'

Bill tried not to swear. It wasn't Helen's fault she had an idiot for a husband.

'I could wake him if it's important?'

'It is.'

'Right.'

He heard the phone being carried up the stairs and then the sound of Jim being shaken. His own name was mentioned, then there was an 'Oh, fuck!'

'Morning, Bill.' A bright and cheery voice. 'You're up early.'

'What the hell do you think you're doing running that story?'

A moment's silence then a throat being cleared.

'The story's true.' Connelly was standing his ground. 'We got it from a good source . . .'

'I know it's true.'

'So . . . what's the problem?'

'The problem is,' Bill took a breath, 'thanks to you these people now know we're on to them. And what do you think they're doing?' Without waiting for an answer, he spat it out. 'They're covering their tracks deleting every pornographic file from here to eternity.'

'Oh.'

'Is that all you can say? "Oh"?'

'I got a call last night. The source was good so I put it in. It filled a slot.'

'It filled a slot! There are weans out there getting their slots filled right this minute.' Bill's voice shook with anger.

'My job is to print the truth.'

'The truth . . .' Bill paused. 'The truth is you've screwed this investigation.'

When Bill reached the office, the story had got there before him. The woman from the university had already phoned wanting to know who had given out confidential information painstakingly gathered over three months. She had been incandescent, Janice said. Whatever they'd found out was useless now.

He spread the paper out masochistically on his desk. *Glasgow Paedophile Ring Nets The Innocent.*

Jim Connelly could certainly write a headline.

14

CHRISSY MISSED RHONA. Tony was all right but after a while you got bored by his tales of holiday conquests and drinking sprees in Mexico, especially if the nearest you would ever get to Mexico was the Mexican restaurant, Amigos.

The change in the weather made her restless. The park below was full of students lounging on the grass in the sunshine, playing music or studying for the year end exams. It made her want to go back to when your only worry was where the next meal was coming from and whether the fifty per cent of the work you'd revised would appear in the exam paper.

Neil had contacted her that morning. He hadn't spent all her money yet, he told her, and he had found out a wee bit about her problem. She laughed because she couldn't believe the money wasn't all gone and because she was nervous talking to him. His voice sounded younger on the phone and he had put on a posh accent and missed out the swear words. He asked her if she would meet him in the park when she got off for lunch.

Chrissy looked at the clock. It was already one o'clock and she hadn't got much done that morning, even less than Tony, who was already away lunching with a waitress from Amigos. He was taking this Mexican thing seriously.

Chrissy told reception she was going out and would be back in an hour.

Neil was waiting for her, sitting on a bench at the bandstand. He waved two paper pokes with a Mackays the Bakers logo on the side.

'Scotch pies and doughnuts,' he said, grinning.

'Fine.'

'And . . .' He produced a bottle from his pocket. 'Vodka and orange. Fresh orange, mind. None of that diluting stuff.' He laughed.

His skin was brown, his eyes dark blue with black lashes. It wasn't surprising the old guys fancied him. Anyone would fancy him.

He munched his way through his pie, handing Chrissy the bottle now and again after wiping it on his sleeve. He had on a white tee-shirt and she could see his neck had healed.

'I've been away for a couple of days,' he said. 'A geezer with a holiday home in the middle of nowhere.' A bleak look crossed his face. 'Not that I got a chance to view the scenery.'

Chrissy didn't want to think about that.

'Here.' He took some money out of his pocket and handed it to her. 'This is yours.'

'Did you find out who sent the letter?'

'Aye.' He'd started on the doughnut now and it seemed to make him thirstier than the pie. 'It's fixed.'

'How?'

'Your brother picked up a guy who recognised him.

He thought Patrick was an easy way to get his dope money. Patrick told him to get lost so he thought he'd try blackmail.' His face hardened. 'I changed his mind for him.'

Relief swept over her. 'Thanks, Neil.'

'Right.'

He looked at her and she suddenly wondered what it would be like to kiss him.

He caught her eye and stopped eating. 'Are you sure about that shag?' he asked, jokingly.

'Neil . . .'

'Aye, right.' He smiled again and stood up. 'I'd better get back to work then.'

'I was going to the cinema tonight,' she found herself saying.

'With your mates?'

'No.'

'Look, Chrissy.' He sat down again. 'Why don't we just cut the crap. I'll meet you after work, we'll go to my place, have a drink, go to bed and then go to the pictures, with maybe a curry in between?'

'All right,' she said, surprising herself.

'No Hail Marys?'

'No Hail Marys,' she agreed.

He shut the curtains but daylight still seeped through, bathing the room in lazy light. The bed sheets were white and when he threw back the covers the whiteness leapt up at her.

'I changed the bed,' he said, reading her face.

Chrissy looked at the bed, then at him.

'Too risky, eh?' His voice was without accusation.

Chrissy ran the risks over in her mind like a good scientific officer.

'I haven't changed my mind,' she said.

He took off his clothes and stood naked while he undressed her. His body was boyish, waist and hips narrow, chest smooth. She felt embarrassed to touch him so she tried to make it into a joke by telling him she hadn't been to bed with anyone since she gave up for Lent a year before.

'Then I'll have to make it worth your while,' he murmured.

He found her mouth and touched it lightly, then slid slowly down, circling her breasts, pulling at her nipples, down to breathe softly against the springy hair until her body rose towards him. Then he lifted her legs and lay between them and his tongue began to explore her. When she called out in pleasure, he pulled himself up beside her.

'Okay?'

'Better than okay.'

He reached under the pillow and pulled out a condom, tearing the packet open with his teeth.

He slipped inside and rocked her like a baby until she cried, the tears running saltily down her cheeks and into her mouth.

'You were right to wait for me,' he said as he wiped the tears away with his thumb. 'I wasn't this good in second year,' and she laughed and cried at the same time.

★   ★   ★

Afterwards he propped the pillows up and they sat side by side watching the breeze teasing the curtain's edge into fluttering motion. Chrissy felt happy. It was an unfamiliar feeling.

'My toes are tingling,' she said.

'I get to the parts other guys can't reach.'

She elbowed him jokingly in the ribs and he made a show of rolling off the bed in agony before padding over to the bathroom. Chrissy folded her hands on her belly and didn't want to be anywhere else.

Chrissy had first opened her legs, as her mother put it, when she was eighteen. It had been a great disappointment. It had been after a dance at the Catholic Social Club with some random guy. Chrissy was fed up saving herself for her future husband. Virginity had lost its currency, however Father Riley whinnied on about hell.

'Stop it.' Neil was peeking round the bathroom door at her, dripping all over the floor.

'What?'

'Thinking.'

He sounded like her mother.

'Come on,' he shouted, heading back into the shower, 'I'll give your back a scrub.'

They stood together, the water parting above their heads and running down their backs. He put his nose to hers and she could see the water on his eyelashes.

'I'm starving,' he said, 'are you ready for that curry or do you fancy another go?'

'You or a poppadom, you mean?' she said.

He caught her eye and bent to lift her nipple into his mouth.

15

'WOW!' RHONA LOOKED round Gavin's study, impressed.

'It's like the *Starship Enterprise* in here.'

A flat wall screen lit up the room, trickling a vertical line of mixed green letters and numbers.

Gavin smiled apologetically. 'I'm a *Matrix* fan.'

He became absorbed in responding to line after line of commands, none of which meant a thing to Rhona.

'You really like this sort of thing, don't you?' she said.

'Sad. Isn't it?' He pulled a face.

'It's not that different from what I do. Find clues and want to know what they mean.'

'Yes, I suppose it is.'

Rhona had broached the subject of making a computer search during their second meal together. When Gavin had asked her out again she had agreed, ignoring the internal voice telling her that finding Liam wasn't her only motive for accepting.

'Maybe we can get to the sweet, this time,' he said. 'The ice cream's great.'

'Sorry.'

'Only joking.'

She had been deliberately vague when she raised the subject, between mouthfuls of blueberry sorbet. If she gave him some information, might he be able to trace someone's current whereabouts?

Gavin transferred his attention from his chocolate chip and banana.

'That depends.'

Her face fell.

'I mean, it depends on what you have to go on and how long you're prepared to search.'

'A name, a date of birth and place of birth. Would that be enough?'

'Might be. Depends how old the person is. If they're paying tax . . .'

'No. This person might not be paying tax.' She was embarrassed. 'Not yet, anyway.'

'Mmm.' Gavin tactfully ignored her evident discomfort. 'Parents paying tax?'

'Probably.'

'If you think this person . . .'

'It's a boy.'

'If you think this boy still lives at home, then we might be able to find him through his parents.'

'Oh.'

'Is there anything that might make him special? Something that would be documented somewhere?'

'Yes. Yes, there is.'

Gavin was explaining how, after they met in the taxi, he'd spent an hour tracking her contact details down on his PC.

'You're on a police file. Did you know that?'

She shook her head.

'You must have been vetted when you got your job.'

'Yes.' She remembered. She'd had to sign some sort of form when she accepted the post at the lab.

'I could have looked at the contents of your bank account if I'd wanted, but I didn't.'

'What?'

'Only joking. Besides, I don't chase women for their money, only for their brains.'

Rhona told him that that was just as well.

'So what have you got?' he said.

Rhona handed him the piece of paper with Liam's date of birth, place of birth and his adopted name.

'This could take a while.'

'That's okay.'

'You want to do the whole thing tonight?'

She realised he had hoped to spend at least part of the evening on other things.

'I'm sorry. If it's a lot of trouble . . .'

He would either do it because he was nice, or because he wanted to have sex with her.

'Okay,' he said and touched her arm. 'But you might as well go home. I'll let you know if I find out anything.'

'I'd rather stay,' she said.

She watched for a while, her chair close to his. At first he explained everything he was doing. He started with the main tax centre in East Kilbride to see if he could find a reference to the adoptive parents in the tax records. When she looked askance, he told her he had clearance because he did cybersleuth work for the police.

'I don't want you to get into trouble.'

He grinned. 'You won't. I'm good at this, re-member?'

As he became more absorbed, he gave up explaining what he was accessing and cross referencing and Rhona drifted off into a light doze. Gavin must have got her to the couch, because she woke up there later, feeling very disorientated.

'Sorry,' she said guiltily.

'Never mind. Come and see what I've found.'

James and Elizabeth Hope had registered the adoption of a child one month after the nurse had removed Liam from Rhona's arms. The baby had been named Chris-topher Liam Hope. Edward was right. Liam had no connection with the murdered student.

Gavin was struggling to smother a yawn and Rhona suddenly realised how tired he must be.

'I'm sorry,' she said, standing up.

'What for?'

'For making you stay up half the night.'

'Is this what you wanted to know?'

She nodded gratefully. 'Thanks.'

He met her eyes speculatively.

'I'll get you a printout.'

There was an awkward moment while they waited for a taxi to arrive.

'I'd appreciate it if you'd write down what you need then tear up the printout.' Gavin looked slightly embarrassed.

'Of course.'

At the front door, Gavin kissed her lightly on the cheek. For a moment Rhona wished she wasn't going home. Then the moment passed. She thanked him and climbed inside the cab. The door was shut and she was alone.

Travelling through the dark and silent city, Rhona thought how quickly Edward had come up with the evidence she'd asked for. When she'd asked how, he'd brushed her off. He was a lawyer. Dealing in legal documents was his business. His voice had been firm but Rhona had detected an underlying note of alarm. She had rattled Edward and he wanted her off his back, fast.

The sky was streaked with dawn as she climbed the stairs to her flat. Her AWOL week was nearly over. She would have to go back to work on Monday, and she would have to admit she hadn't been in France. Turning the key in the lock, Rhona wished Sean was asleep in the big bed and she could climb in and wrap herself round him.

In the gloom of the hall the dot of green light flashed from the phone but she didn't touch the play button. There was already too much to think about. Any messages could wait till morning. There had been a lull of three days since she'd heard from Sean and she wondered if he'd given up on her. Somehow she couldn't bring herself to call him. She had to straighten her head out. And she couldn't do that until she traced her son.

Rhona locked the front door and went through to the empty bedroom. Chrissy's message, delivered in a high-pitched frightened voice, was left unheard.

16

CHRISSY PEERED ALONG the road, praying another taxi would appear over the hill, this time with the orange light on. Two had swept past her in the last fifteen minutes. After the second disappointment she was so agitated she began to walk. Her brain was in overdrive, going over the same ground again and again. She couldn't help it. She kept telling herself it didn't make any difference. She should have told someone about the welts on Neil's neck earlier. Rhona, the police, anyone. But she hadn't. And now it was too late.

She spotted a black shadow in the distance and waved wildly. The taxi disappeared down a dip in the road and when it reappeared fifty yards away, the 'for hire' light was off. Chrissy swore in desperation, convinced it was headed for a phone booking. She was wrong. The taxi drew in and Chrissy said a silent thank you, threw in her bag and climbed in.

'Where to, hen?'

It was eight hours since Neil had spoken to her. He had told her not to go near the flat before midnight. 'You might meet one of the customers,' he said. 'Get a taxi as far as the pedestrian precinct, then walk the rest. If anyone bothers you, tell them to fuck off, but don't go up the entrance if anyone's hanging about. And check for cars. Okay?'

She had listened in silence, her mind turning somersaults because he sounded so scared. That made her scared, too.

'Chrissy?'

'Yes.'

'I'll see you soon. And remember, just sound normal, right?'

'Right.'

She tried. She left work (ignoring Tony's quizzical look), went home, had her tea and said she was going camping for the weekend.

'That's new,' her mother said, giving her a hard look.

Thank God her father and brothers weren't there. It was Friday and they were out on the bevvy, as per usual.

She left the house at nine and went round to a friend's until eleven. Claire was curious about the bag, but Chrissy told her the same story. She was going camping with some mates from work but they couldn't leave until late. She was beginning to believe it herself.

'But how will you manage to put a tent up in the dark?'

'Oh, there's folk up there already,' she lied.

After she left for Neil's, she took it into her head to call Rhona's flat, whatever Neil had said. It wasn't any use. Rhona wasn't back yet.

When Chrissy asked the taxi driver to stop, he looked concerned as he took the fare.

'It's gey late to be walking round here, hen. Will you be all right on your own?'

She made a stupid joke about wandering round the red light district of Glasgow in the early hours of the morning.

'You and half of Glasgow, hen,' he replied with a snort.

Neil's street was empty. Chrissy walked past the entrance as far as the first side road, just as Neil had told her. She relaxed a bit and started to walk slowly back.

A car crept alongside.

'You looking for me?'

She was one door away from Neil's. She swithered. To walk on past might mean this car following her, or . . .

'Come on, doll. Help me out.'

The driver pointed to his bulging crotch.

She shook her head and turned in at the entrance.

'Bitch.' He spat after her.

At least the light had been fixed. Chrissy quickly climbed the stair, hoping the guy in the car wouldn't take it into his head to follow her. Two filled condoms lay in the corner of Neil's landing. This was a regular venue for someone.

Chrissy reached up and swept her fingers along the ledge and found the key where Neil had said it would be. It turned easily in the lock. As she pushed the door open Chrissy heard the click of stilettos in the tenement entrance and a high pitched giggle of anticipation. The guy had struck it lucky.

She quickly locked the door behind her. The package of photographs lay on the mat. She picked it up and shoved it in her pocket.

The windows were tightly closed and the flat was stuffy. Chrissy went straight to the chest of drawers and threw some of Neil's clothes in the bag she'd brought, then went into the kitchen. The bottle of vodka was under the sink and the money was where he'd said, in the Brillo pad box. She shoved the vodka in the bag and the money in her pocket with the photos and headed out.

The panting skirmish on the landing had begun. The woman was against the wall. She caught Chrissy's eye and started to grunt and moan more energetically to hold the customer's attention and cover Chrissy's departure.

Outside, Chrissy passed the black car waiting for its owner's return.

17

EDWARD GAVE FIONA'S hand a squeeze and leaned back against the soft black leather of Sir James Dalrymple's Rolls Royce. Fiona returned the pressure, turning from the view of the rolling Perthshire hills to give him a smile.

Edward touched the leather door with his other hand, admiring the taut shine. He had already opened the walnut drinks cabinet and poured two whiskies, which now sat on the fold-down table, the ice gently pinging the elegant crystal as they swung smoothly round the steep bends on the country road. When Sir James had offered the previous night to send the car for them, Edward had protested it wasn't necessary. Sir James had insisted.

'Nonsense. I shan't be needing it and you might as well travel in comfort. I look forward to seeing you and Fiona at Falblair. The first of many weekends, I hope.'

Edward hoped so too.

June had seen the end of the rain and the start of the summer. Each day dawned clear and blue. The sort of weather that raised spirits and made people happy, despite everything.

Perfect campaigning weather, Edward thought.

'What are you thinking about?'

'Oh, things. The campaign.'

'And?'

'Going well.'

'Urquhart? How's he doing?'

Edward knew what Fiona meant.

'He's at Falblair already,' he said. 'Went up early to discuss campaign finances with Sir James.'

'That sounds good.'

Fiona lifted her glass and sipped her whisky. Edward looked at his wife with pleasure. Her hair had been done recently. It was blonder, he thought. Her face was smooth and evenly-toned, beige against the red lips.

Sensing his desire, she put down her glass and let her fingers brush his swelling crotch.

The car was slowing down, preparing to turn in between two stone pillars topped with ornate gargoyles. A man dragged the black metal gates over the gravel and waved them through. A single-track road wound ahead through rowan, birch and pine. They heard a muffled crash as a roe deer sprang from the woods and jumped lightly across the road in front of them.

'Sir James said Falblair was a hunting estate,' said Edward, delighted. Then he spotted the house and was momentarily lost for words.

The Victorian mansion stood in a wide expanse of parkland. It was an impressive Gothic pile, fronted by a carefully manicured lawn that rolled down to a private loch with a jetty and a moored rowing boat.

Across the loch in the trees, they caught a glimpse of the chimney of an estate building.

'That must be the hunting lodge Sir James mentioned. He rents it out to weekend parties,' said Edward.

'All in all, very nice,' murmured Fiona.

'Indeed,' agreed Edward, secretly wondering how many boards he would have to be on, to get a place like this.

They drew up in front of the magnificent entrance. As the chauffeur opened the car door, Sir James appeared with Ian Urquhart, who looked extremely pleased with himself. It seemed discussions had gone to plan.

Sir James stepped forward to meet them.

'Welcome to Falblair, Edward, and Fiona. How lovely you look, my dear. Quite flushed from your journey through the Perthshire hills. Come in and make yourself at home.'

'The trouble with Scotland is that it's full of Labour supporters!'

Sir James raised an eyebrow humorously, the cue for a ripple of laughter to make its way round the assembled company. 'So, Edward,' he continued. 'It's your job to prove me wrong. Wake up the electorate. Show them they're better off with us.'

They were sitting round a log fire after a delicious meal, served, Edward had noted, by no fewer than three attractive young women. Now he was nursing a fine brandy.

'It's rather like the good old days of the Empire,' Sir James was saying. 'Sometimes the natives don't recognise what's in their own interest.'

Edward joined in the approving nods of agreement.

'They simply don't understand our policies,' Sir James continued. 'That is the reason they reject them.'

Someone let out a snort of contempt.

'It's up to us to go on explaining. Don't worry, as the medicine takes effect, they'll come round.'

'Hear, hear!' Edward chimed in.

'I'm glad you agree, Edward. Your election will be a step in the right direction. Your predecessor was sound enough, but set in his ways. Should have retired years ago. We need fresh blood. This is a tremendous challenge, and I am sure you are the man for the job.' Sir James beamed benificently.

Edward held out his glass for the proffered refill. He could take any amount of this sort of life, he thought. The glorious ambience, the excellent food, the wine, but best of all was the permeating odour of opulence, a mix of silk, brocade and polished wood. Exactly what he'd been trying to develop in his house and would have done, if it hadn't been for the dubious smells that emanated from his children's rooms.

'Enough business for tonight.' Sir James' glance followed Ian Urquhart as he moved to replenish Fiona's glass. 'What about our plans for tomorrow? A shoot for the gentlemen, of course, and . . .' he paused here in admiration at his own magnanimity, 'a morning's pampering at Gleneagles for the ladies.'

There was a murmur of appreciation from the

females, including Fiona, Edward noticed. He had been looking forward to the prospect of some shooting; the cool metal shotgun in his hands, its thrust as he pulled the trigger. Bang. Bang. Bang. Edward glanced over at Fiona and she smiled back at him.

The party was breaking up, drifting towards the wide curve of the staircase. Ian Urquhart came over to ask Edward if there was anything he needed to discuss with him before he went to bed.

'There'll be plenty of time to talk in the morning,' interrupted Sir James. 'I'm sure you're all anxious to get to bed. I should say, Edward, that young Urquhart here has been zealously representing your interests since he arrived. You're very lucky to have him.'

'I believe I am, Sir James. I believe I am.'

Fiona closed the bedroom door firmly behind them.

'Well,' she said.

'Indeed.'

Fiona crossed to the dressing table and began to take off her jewellery. Edward watched her, admiring the curve of her neck in the firelight.

'Sir James could hardly keep his eyes off Ian. I'm sure he got him to refill the glasses so that he could look at his bottom,' she said.

Edward came to stand behind her. He laid his hands on her shoulders, massaging them free of the black straps of her dress. 'I can't blame him for that, Fiona. I've been known to do the same to you.'

Fiona laughed and looked up at him.

'So what do you think? Are they at it?'

'Without a doubt.'

'You're not annoyed?'

'On the contrary, I'm delighted. As long as the romance lasts as far as the by-election.'

'You're a mercenary, Edward.'

'And that's why you love me.' He slid his hand down to hold her breast.

'I could get to like . . .' she waved her arm around the room, 'all this.'

'Just what I was thinking,' Edward said.

'So it all depends on the result of the election.'

It was a statement, not a question.

'The election is a foregone conclusion.' Edward wasn't going to show nerves, even to Fiona.

'I wouldn't like anything to come between us and success,' she said.

'Nothing will.'

18

JONATHAN HAD NOT switched on the computer for two days. Instead he lay across his bed and stared at the ceiling, which had an amazing capacity to transform itself into sets of digital images. When this got too freaky, he went out to buy fags and more drink. When he got back, Mark had left a message on his mobile to ask why he wasn't answering his email, and to say he was in Aviemore and would be back Saturday to tell him all about it. Jonathan didn't want to know.

He got up from the bed, collected four sticky glasses from various sentry points about the room and went down to the kitchen. The kitchen was in as big a mess as his room and he felt marginally guilty that Amy would have to clean it up before his parents came home from their swanky weekend in the country. But, he decided, it wasn't all his mess. Morag and her microwave slimmer's meals! Foil wrappers covered every kitchen surface, curled up in disgust at the remains in their white containers. He had already told the stupid bitch that eating two slimmers' meals was the same as a fat-filled diet.

Jonathan brushed the cartons into the already over-flowing bin and reached in the cupboard for what had to be the last tin of baked beans. He went to look for a clean plate. Small hope. He rinsed the least revolting one under the hot tap, tipped the beans onto it and put it in the microwave. While he waited for the ping, he toyed with the idea of a drink of milk then changed his mind when he saw the age of the carton and settled for a Coke instead.

As he closed his mouth gingerly over the scaldingly hot beans he tried to work out what he should do. It would have to be today. His parents would be back tomorrow. He reached for the Coke and pulled back the ring. The can exploded angrily and some liquid frothed out onto the floor. Fuck. There was a dish towel near the sink and he began mopping up with it, but it was already stiff with the remains of some earlier spillage.

Jonathan gave up and threw it in the sink.

Back in his room he emailed Simon. A reply came almost right away and they arranged to meet outside the Gallery of Modern Art at seven. They would get a taxi and go wherever Jonathan fancied.

It was that easy.

Jonathan shut down the computer and headed for the shower, taking the vodka with him. As the water pounded his head, he sang at the top of his voice. No one banged on the door to tell him to hurry up or shut up.

19

CHRISSY'S MOTHER ANSWERED. She told Rhona that Chrissy had left on Friday night and wouldn't be back till late Sunday.

'What's up, hen? Is everything all right?'

'Fine,' Rhona assured her. 'I just got back from Paris and I really wanted to talk to her. Her mobile seems to be off. Do you have any way of getting in touch with her?'

'Naw, hen. She's gone camping.' Rhona heard the noise of a door slamming. 'I'll have to go, dear. I'll get Chrissy to call as soon as she gets back.'

Rhona's heart sank. She cursed herself for not checking her messages. But what difference would it have made? She hadn't been there to talk to Chrissy.

She went through to the kitchen.

In the convent garden, her friend the gardener was at work raking the path through the rhododendrons. He must have sensed someone watching for he looked up and waved. On a normal morning Rhona would have taken him a coffee. Not this morning.

There was a message from Sean but he had been cut off almost immediately. A second garbled attempt was amputated mid-sentence. Then another voice, scarcely recognisable as Chrissy's.

★   ★   ★

Whatever way she looked at it, Rhona just didn't buy the story of the camping trip. It struck her that Tony might know something. She would give him a call. A sleepy female voice answered.

Rhona apologised. 'Is Tony there?'

'Just a minute, I'll get him.'

'Sounds like I'm cramping your style,' she said when he came on the line.

'No problem. Welcome back. How's things?'

'Fine. Look, did Chrissy tell you where she was going this weekend?'

'No. Should she have?' He paused. 'Wait a minute. There was something. Someone rang her yesterday afternoon and she went a bit funny after that. Said her dad had gone on the rampage again.'

'Right. Thanks. That's probably it.'

'Can I do anything?'

'I don't think so.'

'See you Monday then.'

The post and the newspaper arrived while Rhona was in the shower, still mulling over her next move. She carried them through and laid them on the kitchen table. The postcard showed the Sacré Coeur bathed in warm sunshine.

Dearest Rhona,
Good food, good wine, great music.
Missing you. Phone soon.
Love S.

Her hand was shaking as she put the card down. Sean hadn't given up on her yet. But then he didn't know the truth about her, any more than she knew the truth about him.

Rhona opened the newspaper to find Edward smiling smugly above a full page interview. She skim-read the article.

'Edward Stewart, the acceptable face of new Scottish Conservatism,' Rhona muttered. Even Jim Connelly hadn't cracked the carefully constructed façade. At least Edward wasn't the main headline and that would definitely piss him off.

She glanced over the paedophile allegations, then laid the paper down. She wasn't in the mood to think about the horrors in that story. Then she noticed Bill Wilson's name and picked it up again. This time she read it properly.

20

BILL'S ANGER HAD left him drained. Somehow, this time he had internalised the anger, personalised it, and it wasn't good for either his stomach or his heart, or so Margaret had informed him. He knew it himself.

He also knew he could do nothing about it. The death of this particular boy in these particular circumstances was as near to home as it had ever been, and he couldn't explain why. As well as putting his own blood pressure up, and his wife's, he had also rubbed the kids up the wrong way.

'We can't live in a prison,' his daughter had said after the last row. 'You'll have to let us go back out some time.'

And she was right.

As soon as the exposé on paedophiles hit the newspapers, the cybersleuth team, headed by Gavin MacLean, started reporting problems mapping relevant sites in the investigation. It was as if they had never existed. And they were no further forward on the murder investigation either.

There had been plenty of leads about the curtains, all of them false. No one had reported seeing Jamie in the hours before his death, no one in the close had seen anything. Since most of the occupants were avoiding the law themselves, that wasn't too surprising.

Bill told Janice he was going down to the canteen. He had promised Margaret he would eat regularly if he was going to spend so much time at work.

'We've had a call from Childline you'll want to know about,' Janice said.

Bill realised that the young Constable had been putting as much time in on this case as he had, and that was a hell of a lot.

'Why don't you tell me about it down in the canteen? My treat,' he said, and Janice groaned.

'Some treat.'

They carried the canteen's attempt at vegetable lasagne over to a table and sat down.

Bill looked up from his gloomy study of the contents of his plate to his junior officer. When he was her age, most people had never heard of paedophiles. Now every second week there was a story of abuse. It had been going on all the time. In the old days the kids just didn't tell anyone, because they didn't think anyone would believe them. And they were right.

'The call from Childline . . .'

'Is this going to put me off my lasagne, Janice?'

'Probably.'

Bill pushed the plate away.

'Okay. Let's have it.'

'A boy contacted them. Says he's mixed up in this paedophile ring.'

'Was he genuine?'

Janice nodded. Childline had been sure of it, she said. The boy said he had been recruited by email and he couldn't get out. He had been threatened that pictures of him would be sent to his family if he told anyone.

'The boy sounded pretty desperate, Sir.'

'Have we any idea where he was calling from?'

Janice shook her head.

'Did he give any clues to the identity of any of the men?'

'No. He said they would kill him like the last one, if he gave them away.'

'Bastards.'

'Yes, Sir.'

He needed one lead, just one real lead to get close to these animals. Then he would get them.

'Get hold of Gavin MacLean. See if he can home in on these email connections.'

Janice rose to go, leaving her lasagne to congeal on the plate. Bill looked at her tired face and made her sit back down.

'Eat your food first, Constable. And that's an order.'

'Yes, Sir.'

He stood up. 'I'm going out for a while. I'll be back in an hour.'

The underground car park was almost empty. His dark blue Rover was alone in the far corner. The early shift were all away home. He turned the dial on the radio until he found some background music, then started her up and headed out the gate into the early evening light.

At first he just drove around aimlessly. Driving helped him think. He liked the way both sides of his brain worked at once. One half concentrating on the road, the other busy unpicking knots in the case.

Since Connelly's article on paedophiles, there had been an outcry. It had been what the Super called 'a good public response'. A lot of folk just didn't like their neighbours and would report them for anything. And some people had it in for gays, whether they lived decent lives or not.

The catalogue of complaints had led them nowhere. Whoever the real predators were, they had covered their tracks very well indeed.

Bill headed for Maryhill. When he reached Erskine Street, he pulled over and stopped at number 11, scanning the tenement for the window on the second floor. The window was bleary with grime. In the sunshine, the ragged bit of net that covered the bottom half was the colour of a rainy day.

It was on a day like this, also in June, that he'd left this street for good. His mother had come to that window and waved, determined not to betray a trace of distress. It was what she wanted for him. She'd raised four fine sons in that tenement flat, instilling them with a fierce sense of right and wrong. His brother John was in Canada in the police there. William, the clever one, was a lawyer in Edinburgh, as far away from this place as it was possible to imagine. The second youngest, Kenny, had gone to sea like his father. And then it had been his own turn to leave.

A figure had come out of the tenement entrance and was eyeing him up and down. The boy was streetwise, six going on thirty. He ran at the car and spat on the window, shoving one finger up.

When Bill's mother got ill, she refused to leave Erskine Street and come and stay with Margaret and him, so he got her a home help and they went to see her as often as they could. Bill would sometimes get a police car to go and check on her and she would ask the officers in for a cup of tea. On more than one occasion, weans as young as this one had removed a wheel or a wing mirror while his men sat indoors eating shortbread biscuits.

Bill started the engine and the kid ran up an alley, the single finger still waving defiantly. Bill took one last look and drove away from the broken kerb, glad his mother had never seen things come to this.

He drove back into town. This time he headed for Kelvingrove Art Gallery. He parked on the long leafy avenue. He got out and started to walk.

Men who killed like that never stopped with one. The likelihood was the urge had developed over a period of time, satisfied at first by small acts of violence; then, as it became stronger, the sexual act was only a part of the pleasure; the satisfaction from the violence was the whole. He knew he was already waiting for the next one. Of the four deaths this year, the last two were unsolved. Martin Henderson, the student found in this park, and Jamie Fenton.

Bill ran the first incident over in his mind.

Martin had been seen leaving the Union alone about ten o'clock. The doctor put his death at about midnight. That left two hours unaccounted for. There had been signs of homosexual activity and violent assault. Death had come from a blow to the head, possibly from a blunt instrument, or he could have hit a rock when he fell. They never found the instrument or the rock.

By the time the body was found next morning, the river was topping its banks. Rhona and the scene of crime team had drawn a complete blank. They reached the conclusion that the victim had been cruising for sex and had been jumped. But Rhona had put forward the idea that he might have arranged to meet someone here; that the one he had sex with was the one who killed him.

'Remember the thong with the cross on it?' she had said.

'The Doc said they pulled his head back with it.'

'Yes. He didn't die of asphyxiation, but there was bruising on his neck consistent with having the thong tightened.'

'So if it's the same murderer, why didn't he bite?'

'You and I both know how these acts tend to go through an escalating sequence. Maybe now he needs more.'

'We got nothing on that last one, no trace evidence at all?'

'Only a small amount of the victim's seminal fluid. Nothing from the assailant.'

'If they were having sex, that's unusual.'

'That was my argument last time, Bill. No trace evidence. No sexual encounter. I believe the boy's seminal fluid was ejaculated at the moment of death. We both know that's not unusual.' She paused. 'But now I'm not so sure. When I examined Jamie Fenton, most of the seminal fluid was low down on the thighs. The mouth showed small traces. Dr Sissons said the oesophagus was clear and he found next to none in the rectum.'

'So?'

'Maybe the murderer has problems climaxing. If it's the same man, maybe he didn't reach a climax at all the first time. Maybe that's why he lost it.'

'And with Jamie?'

'I think he strangled Jamie to help him reach a climax and when that didn't work, he bit him.'

'You're beginning to sound like a Forensic Psychiatrist.'

She was silent for a moment. 'We have to try and understand why, Bill. It's the only way we'll get him, before he does it again.'

Neither of them needed a Forensic Psychiatrist to tell them that. Both victims had been students. That could be their link. There was little else left to check out.

When the university authorities got back to him, they told him that Martin Henderson had also been a regular in the computer lab.

He walked on, letting the sound of the river drift through his mind. Then he went back to the car and drove to the station.

Janice was waiting for him. Something had happened. A raid on a local pornographic video dealer had thrown up an unexpected clue. While the team were going through the routine of observing the stuff and noting down any faces they recognised, they'd found a clip featuring Jamie Fenton. Tied to a four-poster bed, his wrists held by a blue plaited cord with tassels hanging from the end.

In the background hung familiar curtains, swirling with colour.

21

JUST AS JONATHAN pulled the front door shut, his mobile rang. It was Mark.

'Want to meet up tonight?

'Can't. I'm going out.'

'Who with?' Mark sounded slightly incredulous.

'Sorry, I'll have to go, or I'll be late.' Jonathan hit the red button, laughing at his mental picture of Mark's face.

On the road to the bus stop he passed Susan Wheatley. She said 'Hi' and looked as if she might stop and speak to him, but he walked on. On another day he would have been over the moon to be singled out by her. But not today. Today he didn't need Susan Wheatley.

The vodka he'd downed before he left made him feel he didn't need anyone. Everything was perfect. The parents wouldn't appear before tomorrow night. Morag was supposed to be in charge, but she was far too busy being shafted by her new boyfriend.

Jonathan sat upstairs on the bus, wishing he'd had a smoke on the way to the stop. He wondered if Simon smoked. He'd never said. He didn't even know what age Simon was. But he wasn't old, that was for sure.

They had been emailing each other for weeks. Jonathan felt he'd told him just about everything he could about what he felt, what he thought. He'd made some stuff up as well. It was easy to talk big on email. Easy to say you'd done this and that, laugh about what really frightened or upset you. Simon always understood. Unlike his family.

He almost missed his stop, he was so immersed in thought. He stood up and pinged the bell. The driver hit the brakes, throwing Jonathan forward.

'Make your mind up sooner next time, son,' he shouted after him.

A group of goths were sprawled on the steps, soaking up the sunshine. Jonathan looked up and down the street. He was dead on time but Simon wasn't there. Disappointment swept over him. Then a tall handsome figure emerged from behind a pillar and called his name. Jonathan smiled and went towards him.

When Jonathan woke next morning, Amy had already arrived. He could hear the sound of the hoover droning across the hall carpet. Amy had the radio turned up and she was singing along loudly and tunelessly.

Jonathan rolled out of bed, waiting for the familiar stab in his head from too much drink, then remembered he hadn't drunk much, after all. Simon hadn't been into getting smashed.

He made for the shower, thinking he would borrow the hoover after Amy was finished and tidy his room. He would even open the window and let in some fresh air.

He stood in the shower, letting the water pound on his head, allowing the tingle to soak through him. Last night had been great. For once he felt like he was actually in the right place, with the right person, saying the right things.

He turned off the hot stream and rubbed himself dry. When his mum and dad came back they would find him out in the garden, mowing the lawn. That should be good enough for a fiver. And there would be an email from Simon. Jonathan's chest tightened at the thought. Simon was cool.

When the car purred into the drive an hour later, Jonathan had started on the lawn. The effort was definitely worthwhile. His father's face was a picture when the chauffeur opened the car door to let him out.

'Well I never. What's got into you?'

'Mum said the grass needed cut. So . . .'

'Your mother's always talking about the length of the grass. It's never spurred you on before.'

'Edward. Don't discourage Jonathan.'

'Oh, and Mum. I've cleaned my room. I borrowed the hoover from Amy.'

'My God. Now I have had a perfect weekend,' said Edward.

'Nice time, then?'

'Very nice. Is your sister here?' Edward glanced about as if Morag would suddenly emerge from the shrubbery.

'She's out with Anthony,' said Jonathan, thinking he'd have to extract a little working capital from Morag later, for not telling them she'd never been 'in' since they left.

His father grunted and went inside while his mum slipped him a ten pound note for cutting the grass.

'I hope you had a nice weekend, Jonathan,' she said, and he wondered if she was going to ask him what he'd done. It didn't matter if she did. He had his story ready.

After dinner, Jonathan took himself off to his den. He'd endured his father's endless anecdotes long enough. Sir James said this, Sir James said that. Who cared?

Now he was lying, his head propped against the grassy slope, having a cigarette. He watched the smoke rise and dissipate in the thick foliage. He was thinking about what had happened.

They'd talked for hours. Jonathan was amazed at how much they'd found to say to one another, especially after all the emails. Simon was older than he'd expected but it didn't matter. He was funny. They'd had a good laugh about school and girls and Jonathan's family. Talking with Simon seemed to stop him feeling so angry about everything.

They'd gone to three different clubs. Everyone seemed to know Simon. Some came over and sat at their table for a while.

Back at Simon's flat it had been a bit awkward. Simon had asked outright if Jonathan wanted to go home and offered to call a taxi right away. But he didn't want to go home.

Jonathan stubbed out the cigarette. He raised his hips and unzipped himself, pulling down his jeans and pants to circle his hips. His cock, released, sprang up. He rolled over, pressing himself hard into the earth. His cock fattened, fighting the pressure. His brain was filling with images of fucking. He drove himself up and down against the ground, breathing heavily in time to the rhythm. He imagined he was shoving it into Shona Seaton. She was shouting to make it harder, deeper, faster. Now he was watching the soft blond hairs of Simon's hand as it lightly brushed his knee and slipped between his legs, cupping his crotch. He burrowed his face in the fallen leaves, sucking the hardness of Shona's nipples even as Simon sucked at the straining shaft of his cock. Then it came, spurt after spurt exploding. His long groan of pleasure died in the earth and his nostrils filled with the smell of rotting vegetation, sweat and spunk.

When Simon had finally called a taxi around midnight, he'd thrust two twenty pound notes into Jonathan's hand and told him to buy himself a new CD with the change from the taxi.

'I'll email you tomorrow. That is, if you want us to meet up again?'

Jonathan had nodded, his heart leaping with the thought that Simon wanted to see him again.

Jonathan sat up and wiped himself with some grass. He pulled up his pants, then wriggled out of the den, brushing the dead grass from his clothes, and headed back to the house to check his mailbox.

When he pushed open the front door, the good-natured atmosphere had evaporated. He could hear his father's voice in the study, sharp with annoyance, and his mother's tense replies. Morag threw him a warning look from the top of the stairs. Jonathan felt sick. What if his father had found his vodka bottle, or worse, the pictures he'd hidden in the jotter?

He stood like a rabbit caught in the headlights. Should he go upstairs and pretend to be out, or just go out again? Then he realised it couldn't be anything to do with him, or his father would have been out in the garden yelling for him before now.

Something else had happened. Something serious, by the sound of things. He looked up. Morag was leaning over the banister melodramatically mouthing 'phone' at him. He looked over at the hall table. The green message light was flashing on the ansaphone.

Jonathan went over and quietly shut the sitting room door. The study was off the sitting room and his parents wouldn't hear anything. He pressed the play button. There was a buzzing silence, then a woman cleared her throat and began to speak in a voice that cracked like she was angry, or had been crying. She was asking his father to phone her immediately about the paperwork he'd given her. She needed to discuss it with him as soon as possible.

They were still at it, his father trying to cajole or explain. Jonathan crept through the sitting room and stood motionless behind the partially open study door and listened.

That was how he found out that somewhere out there, he had a brother.

Jonathan could tell that his father was shaking with rage inwardly, although outwardly he looked calm.

'Can we rely on this woman to keep her mouth shut?' his mother said.

'Yes. Rhona has principles.'

'And I don't?' Fiona came back sharply.

'I didn't mean . . .'

She cut through his apology.

'Why contact you now?'

'It was that murder. Rhona was the forensic scientist on the case. She said the boy looked incredibly like her.'

'God!' Fiona was really rattled. 'You don't think . . . ?'

Edward shook his head vehemently. 'Of course not.'

'Then where is the child?'

'I told you, I don't know. But that wasn't him.'

'How do you know?'

'The dead boy has been identified.'

'Then why did this Rhona phone again?'

Edward walked over to the window, leaving Jonathan's line of sight.

'Well?' Fiona's voice was impatient.

'She has decided to try and make contact with . . . her son.'

Jonathan heard his mother's intake of breath.

'That would be a bad idea, especially now.'

'Do you think I'm not aware of that?' Edward sounded furious. 'I thought I'd capped this, but it seems I haven't.'

Fiona digested that for a moment. 'If she were to go to the papers . . .'

'You don't have to spell it out. Connelly could blow the election for me.'

'That won't happen.' His mother's voice had taken on the decided tone Jonathan knew so well.

'What do you mean?'

'If necessary, I will speak to . . . this woman. I'll explain that our son would be seriously distressed to find out he has a half brother. I'll ask for her support, woman to woman.'

22

A LOW MIST flirted with the waters of the loch, swirling upwards in a freshening breeze. At the far end, the Cobbler dozed on, his outline sharp against the blue sky.

It would be easy to believe they were safe here. Too easy. The breeze was chill on Chrissy's face. She shivered and pulled the tartan rug tighter round her shoulders.

She was sitting near the water's edge, her back to the shore as it rose towards the grass of the camp-site, a straggle of touring caravans and small tents spaced well apart. Their tent was pitched on a carpet of springy grass around an old rowan.

She fetched the can, filled it with water and stood it on the fire.

She saw Neil top the grassy edge then duck quickly down the bank. When he saw her, the troubled look left his face. He'd got a loaf and some bacon from the camp shop.

He fetched the frying pan and settled it beside the water can.

She watched him as he foutered about, laying the bacon carefully in strips, poking wee sticks in to build the fire; checking the water, then dropping in two tea bags. When he handed her a mug of tea, their hands met. He stroked her fingers.

'All right?' he said, sitting beside her. She nodded. 'After breakfast, I'll take you for a walk.'

While they sat and ate in silence, the sun broke through the mist.

After getting Neil's things from the flat, Chrissy had gone straight to the bus station. She'd had to hang around until her bus came first thing in the morning.

There were no other passengers apart from a woman with two weans, who went up the back and sat between them to keep the peace. Chrissy sank into the front seat, rolled her jacket up for a cushion, and went straight to sleep. When she woke, Glasgow had gone.

'Are you right then?'

Neil had taken the dishes down to the water's edge and washed them. He brought them back up and stacked them to dry near the fire, put on a couple of big pieces of wood and moved his refilled water can to one side. Now he was ready to go.

'Come on.'

He pulled her up, squeezing her hand. 'We'll head up the way. There's a rare view.'

The path skirted the loch for ten minutes, then they took a left up through the trees. All Chrissy could see for a while was the steep path ahead and the back of Neil's tee-shirt, where tiny wee flies clung on, grabbing a lift up the hill. Several times he stopped and waited for her to catch him up. Then suddenly the trees were gone and the air freshened. The path moved among boulders and clumps of heather. They jumped a burn and followed the path round a curve in the hill, and there it was. The vast expanse of the loch stretched beneath them, sparkling into the distance.

'Fucking magic.' He was grinning at her. 'Well?'

'It's fantastic,' she said.

'Aye. Fucking fantastic.'

He pulled her down beside him and pointed round the landmarks and gave them their names. He was talking to her but his eyes were on the loch, caressing each curve of the water, each change of shoreline.

'I used to come here when my dad threw a wobbler. I would hitch a lift up and go back when the money was done.'

'I didn't know you liked all this.'

'Aye, well. A tent's a great place for a shag.'

'Don't joke about it.' Her voice was tense.

'I wasn't joking.'

When he kissed her, his mouth was still salty from the bacon.

'D'you want to walk further up or go back down?'

'Maybe we should work out what to do,' she said seriously.

He shook his head, his face stubborn.

'I know what I'm going to do.'

'What?'

'I'm going to take off all your clothes and I'm going to stare at you until you beg me to shag you.'

'Then you'll wait forever,' she said.

'Some things are worth waiting for.'

On the way back down they passed two men on the track. They were kitted up with climbing boots and rucksacks.

'Yahs,' Neil muttered under his breath.

'They're just walkers like us.'

'They folk think they own Scotland.'

'Maybe they just like it here.'

'Aye. And they'd like it a whole lot better if none of *us* lived here.'

He walked off ahead. The encounter had rattled him and he didn't want her to know. But it was too late.

She could tell he was thinking about the men who had arrived at the flat to 'discuss' the little problem of some photographs. Photographs Neil had sworn he didn't have. Photographs that could incriminate a number of prominent citizens. The same photographs Chrissy had collected and brought here with her. His safety net, Neil called them. If anything happens to me, he'd said, those photos get published. That's why they won't do any more than threaten me. But they came to the flat, they knocked you about, she said. And that's why I came here, he replied. Out of sight, out of mind. I'll go back once things blow over.

He knew she had to catch the eight o'clock bus. After they'd lain in the tent and talked and made love he stirred up the fire and cooked sausages and beans. She said she would come back next weekend.

'No.'

Chrissy felt her stomach lurch.

'But . . .'

'Things'll have blown over. I'll be back in Glasgow by then.'

'To the flat?' She was incredulous. 'But they'll know you're there.'

'I can't afford to miss my regulars.' He avoided her eyes.

She tried to disguise her sense of horror but he drew back, defensively.

'This is what I am,' he said sharply.

'But that man tried to strangle you . . .'

'Things got heavy. It happens sometimes.' He was trying to convince himself as much as her. 'It's the only way they can come.' He turned away. 'It's pathetic.'

She felt sick.

'Then stop it.'

The anger left his face and he touched her cheek. 'You want me all to yourself.'

'I want you to be safe.' Her voice had dropped to a whisper.

'I am safe,' he said firmly. 'HIV negative. Money in the bank. With an insurance policy.' He patted his jacket pocket.

She wanted to argue with him, tell him he must stop doing this to himself. But his look, a mixture of anger and pain, silenced her. She crawled into the tent to get her bag. When she came back out, he behaved as if nothing had happened. He was too good at that, she thought.

'Right then?' he said.

She nodded, feeling defeated.

'You're crazy,' she said.

'You like crazy,' he answered.

There were people at the bus stop and they couldn't talk. His face was a mask. Her chest hurt at the thought of leaving him. Before she climbed on the bus, they kissed hard.

'I'll phone you, right?' he said.

On the way home she tried to work out when it had happened. When having sex had turned into making love. For all his joking talk about shagging, Neil had taken his time, fine-tuning her. She had thought cynically that it was because he'd had so much practice. Now she felt sure that had nothing to do with it. No one takes such care of something that has no meaning.

23

'WE'LL HAVE to tell Bill.'

'I can't.'

'But it could be the same man. He could kill Neil.'

'Don't!'

Rhona had never seen Chrissy vulnerable like this before. They had both arrived at work early on Monday morning. One look at Chrissy's ashen face and she had shunted her into the back lab and shut the door.

'Bill is a decent man and a good policeman. He would protect Neil.'

'No!' Chrissy was adamant. 'I promised I wouldn't tell anyone.' She was close to tears. 'I should never have told you.'

Rhona took Chrissy's hand in hers. 'You were right to tell me. You were braver than me, anyway.'

'What d'you mean?'

'I've got a few secrets of my own. I didn't go to Paris with Sean. I was here all the time.'

'What happened?'

'Things are, well, awkward between us. I saw him with a woman. I asked him if he was sleeping with her.'

'What did he say?'

'He told me it didn't matter if he was.'

'That doesn't mean he's . . .'

'Why didn't he just say no?'

'You wouldn't believe him anyway.'

'Then Edward . . .'

'Edward?'

So Rhona told her everything.

'He asked me to keep quiet because of the by-election.'

'The slimy bastard! And he comes over so charming.'

'Oh, Edward's charming,' Rhona assured her, 'as long as he's getting his own way.'

'I hope you told him to get fucked.'

'Not exactly.' Rhona almost smiled at Chrissy's indignation. 'I kept thinking about it.' She looked desperate. 'And then there was the murder. The boy had a birthmark just like Liam's.'

'Christ! You don't think . . .?'

The words came pouring out now. How both the doctor and the Sergeant had commented how much the boy looked like her, and then Bill, and the birthmark being in exactly the same place.

'Your own DNA, you could check it against . . .'

'Everything's recorded, you know that. How do I explain checking my own DNA?'

'So what did you do?' Chrissy asked.

'Edward made all the arrangements at the time. I phoned him and told him I wanted to know where our son was.'

'I bet he shat himself.'

Rhona managed a laugh.

'He sent me Liam's adopted name to prove it wasn't the dead boy.'

'If I was you, I'd tell the newspapers. They'd love a story like that.'

'I couldn't.'

'No, you couldn't. The same way I can't say about Neil.'

'This man who hurt him. What if he's the killer?'

'Neil says it's all part of the game. It's what they pay for.'

'Did he say anything else about this man? What he looked like? Anything that might link him to the investigation?'

'No. Only that the guy had money. When I asked him to report it Neil said the police wouldn't believe someone like him.'

Rhona spent the rest of the day concentrating on the fibres found on the jeans, while Chrissy worked on the curtain, looking particularly for traces of the previous victim.

It's a long shot, she told Chrissy, but if the killer used the curtain in his routine, it's a chance. If we can match the first victim's DNA profile to the samples we've collected from the curtain, bingo.

Under the microscope the fibres from the jeans turned out to be of two types. One was easily identifiable as dark blue wool. The dye would take spectrometry or chromatography to identify. The remaining fibres were also natural. The boy was wearing cotton jeans and a tee-shirt, but these fibres were cultivated silk.

Rhona looked up from the microscope, a picture of the killer forming in her mind.

He had money. He liked natural fibres next to his skin. He bought silk shirts and ties; pure dark blue wool jackets or trousers. He wore expensive cologne. He could be blond or dark. For him, sex had to be violent. How many men in Glasgow matched the description, assuming he even lived within the city boundaries?

'I think you'd better have a look at this.'

The large sheet of filter paper they'd covered the curtain with had a number of purple patches on it, each identifying a semen deposit.

'The curtain's had a busy time of it,' Rhona said.

'I'll cut out the relevant bits and make extracts.'

'What about old blood?'

Chrissy pointed to two dry filter papers. Each had been activated by the reagents phenolphthalein, alcohol and hydrogen peroxide to produce a pink coloration.

'The spotting was small apart from the blood stains left by Jamie Fenton's injuries,' said Chrissy. 'If the violence is escalating the spots may have come from previous small lacerations, caused by flaying, scratching, that sort of thing.'

'The curtain seems to have been important to the killer. Why did he leave it behind?' Rhona said. 'He must have known it might hold clues to his identity.'

'Something or someone disturbed him?'

It seemed logical. Men who kill during or after sex usually have a routine. A structure they keep to. Their victims were mere commodities. More expendable than a piece of material, thought Rhona. The killer would not have left the material behind unless he had to.

'Oh, and the chemical analysis came through on the paint flake I found inside the boy's pocket. It came from layered paint, the older leaded type. Maybe he had been somewhere where old domestic paint was being stripped down?'

'That could apply to any number of student flats,' Rhona said despondently.

'What about the curtain tie-back?'

'Trace elements of the dead boy, flakes of skin and spots of the victim's blood. Nothing else.'

'Without a suspect, we're working in the dark,' Chrissy said.

'I know and I'm already getting grief about the extra time we're spending on this case. Nobody wants to foot the bill for it.'

'Does Bill know that?'

'No. And I don't plan to tell him. He's already got the Super on his back since the newspaper exposé. Let's just hope Bill can trace the curtain, and soon.'

The rest of the day passed uneventfully. Tony didn't notice his colleagues' preoccupation, his own mind being elsewhere. At lunchtime he went off to meet his Mexican girlfriend for a walk in the park.

Immediately he left, Chrissy began to probe again.

'What are you going to do about your son?'

'I told Edward I'm going to try and find Liam.'

'What did he say?'

'He kept on about the by-election. He's got a good chance. It was a safe Tory seat before the general election and nobody expected it to swing to Labour. And he's got big backers. He mentioned Sir James Dalrymple.'

'This Gavin thing. It's not serious, is it?' asked Chrissy suddenly.

Rhona didn't answer.

'You haven't slept with him?'

'No!'

Chrissy gave Rhona an appraising look. 'You've thought about it. Right?'

She waited for an answer and when none came she didn't lay off. 'What about Sean?'

Rhona shrugged. It was possible to put Sean out of her head when he wasn't around. If they split up, he would survive. There were plenty of others waiting to take her place.

'I think you're wrong about Sean,' said Chrissy. 'Okay, he does like women. But the way he looks at you is different.' Chrissy searched for words.

'Well?' said Rhona.

'Don't take this the wrong way.' Chrissy hesitated. 'It looks to me like you don't want anyone to come too close. Like you don't trust anyone except yourself.' She looked apologetic, but she carried on. 'I used to think it went with the territory. You had to behave like that, to be taken seriously in this job. Maybe you take that through into your life.'

'That's great, coming from you!'

'I know what it's like to be like that.' Her voice tailed

off. She came over and stood beside Rhona. 'Neil's a bit like Sean. Thinks he's God's gift. But he makes me laugh and he doesn't ask me for anything.'

The phone rang in the background.

It was Gavin. Would she like to come round for dinner that evening?

He had something to show her. Something important.

24

WHEN RHONA ARRIVED at Gavin's flat at eight o'clock, she got no answer from the buzzer. She stepped back from the front door and looked up at the second floor window, wondering whether she was too early. The curtains were closed on the big bay windows and the electric light was on, despite the summer evening. Gavin was there all right.

Rhona buzzed again, and this time he answered right away.

'Come on up. But be warned. I've just got out of the shower.'

Rhona stepped into a hallway filled with the delicious smell of garlic, olive oil and warm French bread. Instantly her mouth began to water and she realised with a pang of guilt that she hadn't opened the door to such a delicious smell since Sean left.

He was standing at the cooker, stirring briskly at a pot, a large bath towel tied round his middle. When she walked in, he turned and smiled, while his hand kept on stirring. He was obviously an expert cook.

'The sauce needs me,' he explained.

'Can I help?' Rhona asked, finding it hard to keep her eyes off his naked torso.

'You mean so I can go and get dressed and you can stop feeling embarrassed?'

'Yes,' she admitted.

'Okay. Come here.'

She went over. He took her hand and guided it to the spoon.

'The secret's in the stirring,' he said. 'You must keep a steady rhythm, then quicken as it comes to the boil. It needs two minutes like this.'

She felt his breath on her neck and nodded without speaking.

'Right.' He released her hand. 'I'll go and get some clothes on.'

By the time he came back the sauce was ready, and she had lifted it clear of the gas.

He peered into the pot and gave her the thumbs up.

'Perfect. I hope you're hungry.'

'Mmm.'

'Good. Because I've dragged myself away from my computer to do all this. I even engaged the experts at the local off-licence in my choice of wine.'

She returned his grin.

He pulled out a chair at the carefully set table and tucked it in beneath her.

'Now the wine.'

'You said you had something to show me,' she reminded him.

'That can keep until after dinner. Contrary to popular opinion I don't want to spend all my time in front of a screen. And I don't always want to talk to people electronically.'

She laughed. 'Sorry,' she said.

'That's okay.' His hand brushed hers as he filled her glass. 'Did you walk here?' She nodded.

'Good. Because I bought two bottles of this on special offer.'

She took a sip.

'They're very persuasive at the off-licence,' she said.

'God. You don't like it.' His face took on a mock stricken expression.

'No. No.' She laughed. 'It's fine. In fact it's very good.'

He passed her the salad.

'Let's get started then.'

By the time they reached the coffee stage Gavin had made her laugh at least half a dozen times and she'd told him in detail why she enjoyed her job so much. He had said much the same about his own.

'It's the finding out,' he said. 'The way, if you poke about long enough, a pattern emerges. A pattern that tells a story.'

Gavin was just like her, she thought. The way he went at things. He enjoyed solving problems. Not like Sean, who never saw any to solve. She felt guilty at her harsh thoughts about Sean. In all fairness she couldn't criticise him for the very thing she'd liked about him when they first met. His dreamy acceptance of everything.

'Hey!' Gavin said. 'You're miles away.'

She apologised.

'Are you ready to see what I've found?'

'More than ready,' she said, eagerly.

She followed him into his study.

'I located a list of adoptions around the date you gave me,' he said in a business-like voice. 'All the children come from the Glasgow area and have passed their sixteenth birthday, so they would be able to look for their natural parents, provided they knew they were adopted.'

A list of names rolled up. Her heart in her throat, Rhona began to scan. One name after another. Boys, girls, all unwanted. Given away by their mothers.

Women like her.

'Are you all right?' Gavin was asking her.

She nodded, wondering if all the others had forced themselves to forget, like she had. Made new lives, lives that had no place for a child.

His name and address was near the bottom of the first page. It jumped out at her, as if it too had been searching. Rhona traced each letter intensely, committing the address to memory.

'You've found it?' Gavin took her hand in his.

'Yes,' she said. 'I've found him.'

Gavin's mobile buzzed. He muttered an apology and went through to take the call in the kitchen.

Liam had been adopted by James and Elizabeth Hope, of 19 Warrender Park Street, Glasgow, on 3 February 1985. Such a long time ago, yet no time at all.

Rhona thought back over those years. The terrible despair, six months of punishing herself and Edward for the decision they had made. When he left she was relieved. She didn't have to see his irritated face any more. She had gradually pulled her life back together.

And it worked, up to a point. The guilt began to fade and regret flowed in to take its place.

And all the time, she realised, she had been waiting. Waiting for this moment, when she would find her baby again.

Rhona reached out and clicked on the printer icon, but the printer remained silent. Then a box appeared on the computer screen, stating that printing had been interrupted, and to please replace the paper tray. Rhona pulled the tray out and pushed it back in firmly.

Success.

The green light came on, the printer shunted into life, and the precious printout emerged.

Rhona picked it up and stared at the address. It was so near. Only twenty minutes from where she was right now. Her insides turned over with excitement. If she wanted to, she could go and see Liam. Stand outside his house and watch for him. She could fill the emptiness of those years with the sight of him. She began to plan, not daring to promise herself that she would actually do it. Deep down, knowing it was wrong, that she should wait for him to come to her.

Another piece of paper had dropped into the tray. Rhona picked it up and glanced at it, thinking it must be a second page of names.

But it wasn't.

Her eyes dropped from the inscrutable lines of code at the top to the message at the bottom.

The nightmare closed over her again.

                    *   *   *

Rhona read the words over and over. They conjured up something she could barely grasp. Something horrible. Rhona felt sick. It couldn't have anything to do with Gavin, she told herself. Not Gavin. It was impossible.

But was it?

She thought about the times they had spent together. The way he looked at her, his obvious disappointment when she'd wanted to go home. He had never pressured her. But she knew he wanted her. Tonight in the kitchen, when they were stirring the pot together, his hand on hers. They had both wanted more of the rhythm, the closeness. If she gave the smallest sign, it would happen.

And all that stood for nothing!

She felt stunned at what she had seen on the second printout. Could he really be one of those men? Men like that sometimes had girlfriends, wives, children. Rhona refused to pursue those thoughts any further. She would not believe it of Gavin. He had helped her find her son. He had been patient and understanding.

But Gavin could find anything on the Internet he wanted. He had told her so himself. He had used that knowledge to find out information for her.

Information she shouldn't have access to.

Rhona heard Gavin's conversation end, then the fridge door opened and there was the clunk of a bottle being removed.

'More wine?' he called through.

This is ridiculous, Rhona told herself firmly. It was

Gavin's job to find out these things. Didn't he work for the police?

The voice was nearer now. 'Or do you fancy a liqueur?'

Rhona frantically shoved the two pieces of paper in her pocket.

'That would be nice,' she called back, her voice shaking slightly.

'Well, which would you like?' Gavin's smiling face appeared in the doorway. 'Whisky, brandy . . .'

'Whisky, please.'

He looked at her oddly, his head a little on one side.

'But I'll really have to go soon,' she said.

'I'd better get my skates on, then.'

He reappeared almost immediately and handed her a large glass.

'I'll get you a printout to take with you,' he said.

'No!' Rhona swallowed her panic. 'I've copied the name down already.'

'Where?'

He looked puzzled. She patted her pocket.

'Right.' He was staring at her. 'Let's go and sit in the comfortable seats.'

'I'm sorry, Gavin. I really will have to go.'

'Rhona. It's okay, you know . . .' Gavin's voice tailed off and Rhona felt suddenly sorry for him. She was being an idiot, she told herself. Why not ask him straight out and get the truth, then they could go back to the way they'd been.

But it was no use.

'Thank you for a lovely evening,' she said firmly.

'I'll walk you home if you like,' he suggested. He sounded genuinely disappointed.

'No. Sorry, I need to think.'

At least this time she was telling the truth.

He was watching her intently; this man, who in the space of a second had turned from a potential lover to a potential monster.

'I understand,' he said. 'Let me phone for a taxi then.'

'I'd rather walk. It's not far.'

When they reached the door, he bent and kissed her forehead and his lips felt cold against her skin.

'I'll be in touch,' he said.

'Right.'

He held the door open and Rhona walked quickly towards the stairs. The sound of her heels echocd in the entrance, reminding her of the murder flat, the smell of sweat and semen and violence and death. And something else. An expensive cologne.

25

THIS CALIGULA WAS a twisted bastard.

He could see why he'd chosen the name. Bill remembered the television series about Roman Emperors. They had all been cruel. The one called Caligula had outdone them all for viciousness. The way of the flesh was his major passion.

'So we know one of them calls himself Caligula.'

'Yes,' said Janice.

'Anything else?'

'Childline says there's another one called Simon who does the recruiting. He befriends boys over the Internet. Meets them. Persuades them into having sex. Takes photos secretly, then threatens to show the pictures to their parents. The kids are terrified. Then he introduces them to other members of the group.'

'And where does Caligula fit into this?'

'Apparently Simon told the boy that Caligula likes his sex a bit rough.'

'Okay.' Bill fought back the rising bile. 'Can we get the kid to give us a contact number? Email, phone number, address, anything?'

'Childline say he only phones when he's really

terrified, Sir. He won't answer any questions. Just tells them things and rings off.'

'Does Gavin MacLean know the latest information?'

'Yes. I passed it on to him.'

'What did he say?'

'He'd intercepted emails between a Simon and a Caligula, though chances are, he says, that the names will have changed already.'

'Anything else?'

'Yes, Sir. We have six names of people who bought curtain material through the Paris shop. We're checking on them now. And Sir, I think you should know. One of them is Sir James Dalrymple.'

The call from the Superintendent came five minutes after Bill authorised a call to Sir James. It was obvious Sir James had not wasted much time in getting in touch with his golfing partner. The Super told Bill he understood it was important that he pursue all lines of enquiry but he had it on Sir James's authority that the material in question had not in fact been used in his home, after all. He'd decided against it. A bit too florid for a bachelor's residence. It was given to a church sale a year ago.

'Which church, Sir?'

'He doesn't remember.' There was a tutting sound on the line. 'So,' a pause, then, 'you won't need to bother Sir James any more for now, Bill. He'll be out of the country for a couple of weeks after the by-election tomorrow.'

No, thought Bill. It certainly wouldn't be convenient for Sir James to be interviewed on this matter.

'Let me know if anything else comes up.'

'Of course, Sir.'

The Super had a shittier job than he had, Bill decided. He had to play golf with the likes of Sir James Dalrymple.

Bill Wilson had nothing, less than nothing really. Even so he had the feeling. His guts told him. And his guts always knew first.

Fiona was gratifyingly delighted at the forecast that Edward might better the last Labour majority.

'That would be a kick in the teeth for that Labour chap, what's his name?'

'George Rafferty.'

'Horrible little man.'

'Fiona.'

'Well, it's true.' She pouted at him from above. 'Pour me a drink, Edward. I'm almost ready.'

She disappeared, leaving a heady whiff of perfume. Edward took a pleasurable breath and went through to the sitting room.

Amy had refilled the decanter with the whisky Sir James had given him. He poured two glasses of the golden liquid and walked through the French windows into the garden. It was a glorious evening to sit outside. The herbaceous border was bright with blossoms. He noticed that the gate from the garden into the woods was standing open. He thought about a quiet walk down by the river to recharge his batteries before tomorrow. He hadn't been down there for a while. It had been his favourite spot at one time.

Edward's thoughts drifted back to a particularly luscious dalliance with a legal secretary. She used to bring his papers to the house for signing and always had time for a stroll through the woods.

'Penny for them!'

'Oh, just thinking how glad I am you found this place for us.'

'Yes. It is rather nice.' She followed his gaze across the garden. 'But that's what I'm good at,' she smiled, 'discovering things.'

Edward looked at his wife sharply. It was always difficult to tell exactly how much Fiona knew. Ever since they had it out over Jennifer (the first one after their marriage), she had given him the impression that she didn't want to know. They made a good partnership. She expected him to go far and she intended to go with him. Fiona accepted that power enhanced men's appetites.

They had never spoken of his dalliances again.

'Fancy a stroll?' he asked, thinking longingly of his favourite tree.

'No.' Fiona settled herself in the cushioned chair. 'Let's just sit and relax.' She lifted her legs onto the matching stool. The flimsy material of her dress parted, revealing her slender calves.

'I want to tell you,' she began, 'about my conversation with your little friend, Rhona MacLeod.'

Whenever Edward had to deal with Rhona, his mind seemed to seize up. Alarmingly, something resembling a conscience would begin to surface. Normally he could suppress any such symptoms, especially when

Fiona was voicing the well-rehearsed arguments he fed himself. But this particular subject was different.

Edward had never doubted that adoption was the right decision. Rhona would not consider abortion. But the 'what if?' scenario still insinuated itself. What if he had married Rhona? What if they had kept the child?

Fiona interrupted his reverie.

'She told me to forget it. She'd found out what she wanted to know and she was surprised you had discussed "the incident" with me at all.' Fiona's voice rose in righteous indignation.

Edward could imagine Rhona's reaction to Fiona knowing about Liam. It made him wince.

The adoption had always been between the two of them. It's our baby, Rhona would say, emphasising the word 'our'. We have to decide. So they had decided (Edward liked to pretend it was fifty-fifty), and told no one. How it had hurt Rhona not to tell her precious father. For him to have told Fiona would be a betrayal in her eyes. Well, what did she expect? Fiona was his wife.

'I told her there were no secrets between us,' Fiona was saying, raising her elegantly plucked eyebrows at him, 'and I suggested that it was in everyone's interests that the matter go no further.'

'What did she say to that?'

'She said, "Really?" and hung up.'

Edward took a sip of his whisky. He had no idea how Rhona could have found out where the baby had gone, or even if she had. Either way, he was sure she would tell no one else.

26

THE ROW WAS the usual one.

Money.

Chrissy got up from the table and took her plate to the sink.

'Go on, Chrissy. Just a fiver.' Joseph's wheedling tone made her want to slap him. Of all her brothers, Joseph was the most persistent cadger.

'You heard what she said, Joseph.'

Her mother, the eternal peacemaker.

'Chrissy has no more until pay day.'

Blessed are the peacemakers for they shall inherit the Kingdom of God.

'I don't think so.' Joseph's expression changed to a sneer. 'I heard she's got other sources.'

'What d'you mean?' Chrissy glared at her brother.

Joseph was like a circling dingo, not quite brave enough to strike.

'You know what I mean. Who I mean.'

Chrissy took a quick look at the door and imagined herself walking silently through it. Joseph could not, would not do this to her.

She was wrong.

'Chrissy's new boyfriend rents out his arse for a living.'

'Joseph!' Her mother was horrified. 'What are you talking about?'

Forgive me, Father, for I have sinned.

'I'm saying,' Joseph shot a vicious look at his sister, 'your precious little Miss Whiter Than White is having it away with a well known rent boy of this city.'

'A rent boy? What does that mean, Chrissy?' Her mother looked at her pleadingly.

'Forget it, Mum. He's lying. He always lies when he needs money.'

'Is that right?' Joseph's voice was triumphant. 'Well, ask her who she went camping with and what was going on in the fucking tent.'

'Stop it!' shouted Chrissy.

'Did you ask him where it had been before it got to you?' Joseph's face twisted in malice.

'Don't, Joseph. Please don't,' Chrissy whispered.

Her mother was looking on with incomprehension. Then, with a huge effort, she said, 'You go upstairs, Chrissy. I'll come up in a wee while.'

Chrissy climbed the stairs like an automaton. If Joseph was prepared to tell her mother, he would tell her father too. Once he found out, the house would descend into bedlam. It would all come out about Patrick as well. Her father would ban him from the house. Her mother would be destroyed.

Chrissy lay down on the bed and stared up at the ceiling. Since Patrick left, her home had become a prison. She only chose to stay on because of her mother. She could not abandon her.

Your duty as a good Catholic daughter is to obey your father.

Eventually the talking downstairs stopped and Chrissy heard the back door slam. Her mother must have found some money for Joseph. It was the only thing that would get rid of him.

A tap on the door brought her eyes from the ceiling. Her mother asked quietly if she might come in. She had been crying. All her life, Chrissy had tried not to make her cry.

'Is there somewhere you can go tonight?' she was asking, sitting beside Chrissy on the bed.

Chrissy nodded wordlessly.

'Will you go to this lad?'

'I . . . I don't know if Neil's in Glasgow. I could go to Dr MacLeod. Rhona would let me stay.'

She watched her mother wince with embarrassment.

'I don't know what your father will do when Joseph tells him.' Her mother was smoothing invisible creases from her skirt.

'It's okay, Mum,' she said wearily. 'I know where to go.' She patted her mother's shoulder.

'Are you sure you'll be all right?'

Chrissy nodded. 'Don't worry about me.'

27

IT WAS NINE o'clock and still light. The day had been hot and there was a smell of rain in the air.

Chrissy hitched her bag over her shoulder and set off.

A bus appeared in the distance. It would take her near the city centre. She would go to Neil's flat. If he wasn't there, or if he wouldn't let her stay (Chrissy could not think of that happening), she would go to Rhona's.

Neil's street was deserted. There were no cars parked outside and none passed as she walked along. The entrance had been washed out. Strings from a distintegrating mop still clung to the shiny stairway and there was a pungent reek of disinfectant.

Chrissy coughed a few times in case the woman she'd seen before was already at work, but there was silence from the landing above.

When she reached Neil's door she paused, unsure. What if he was with someone?

Neil had sex for money. Neil had sex with her. No. Neil loved her. There was a difference between having sex and making love, she told herself.

Chrissy knocked hard, then reeled back as the door

swung open under her hand and a sickening stench filled her nostrils.

The gas fire was hissing furiously and the room was like an oven. Covering her nose, Chrissy went over to the window and opened it before turning off the fire. Only then did she brace herself to look more closely at the source of the smell.

The bed was a mass of blood and vomit. She crossed to the bathroom. The door opened with a sucking sigh, fighting the draught from the window. Under her feet lay a film of pink water. She mouthed a prayer before pulling back the shower curtain. Water dripped into an empty bath. Someone had washed themselves in here. Someone who was bleeding badly.

She went back to the living room and followed the bloody footprints to the kitchen, all the time praying, to whom or what she didn't know, the words tumbling over themselves.

Forgive me, Father, for I have sinned, Hail Mary full of Grace. Please God don't let him be dead.

She pushed open the kitchen door. A bottle of vodka stood on the draining board, the cap beside it. Someone had drunk straight from the bottle, leaving a faint pink hand print on the glass.

She knew it was wrong. She knew she should leave everything as it was. But to get the police involved would only make things worse for Neil.

She stripped the bed, put the sheets and pillowcases in a bin bag and took them downstairs to the street. It had started raining. She went back up and found some disinfectant and wiped the watery bloodstains from the bathroom and the kitchen. Then she found clean sheets in the drawer and remade the bed. She kept the window open, ignoring the raindrops that skited over the sill and landed on the carpet.

When she had done everything she could think of, she sat down on the sofa to wait. She wanted to be there for him when he got back.

Chrissy opened her eyes.

Dawn was touching the rooftops. She jerked up and examined her watch. It was five o'clock. The hum of a diesel cab traced down the street. That was what had woken her, she realised. The room was cold now, but at least it smelt fresh. She pulled the window shut and let the curtain fall back.

It was then she heard someone at the door.

Chrissy moved quickly, making for the bathroom. She slipped in and stood behind the door, crushed herself against the wall and peered through the crack. She heard the front door open, then shut, and then there was silence. Someone was standing in the hall. Then the living room door was pushed open and the light came on.

'Jesus, Mary and Joseph.'

'Neil.'

'Christ, Chrissy, you scared me!'

She ran over to him. He winced as he drew her into his arms, but he burrowed his face in her hair, then slid his mouth over hers. He tasted of blood and she pulled back. His face was like pummelled beetroot. One eye was completely closed. There was a white bandage under his shirt.

'What have they done to you?'

'I'm okay. It's not that bad. Believe me,' he tried to make a joke of it, 'I was the good looking one in A&E.'

Somehow the swollen mouth managed a smile. She helped him over to the bed, hearing herself mutter crooning noises as if he was a baby. He lowered himself down.

'Lie beside me,' he said and took her hand.

She started to cry.

'Don't, Chrissy. It's okay. Sshh, now.' He stroked her hair. 'They won't come back. The bastards think they've shut me up. They came for the photos and they had to have their fun as well.'

'Did you give them the photos?'

'Oh aye, I handed them over all right.' He winced as he turned towards her. 'But they bastards didn't get what I know.'

'What d'you mean?' She sat up.

'I know where that curtain comes from, Chrissy. I know where it comes from.'

'You're going to go to the police?'

He shook his head. 'I don't need to. All I need to do is shop them. I'm going to see that newspaper man, Connelly. He'll listen.'

Chrissy was overwhelmed with terror. All she could think about was the next time they came for him. To shut him up for good.

'Wheesht, Chrissy. They won't know it's me.'

Chrissy knew that was ridiculous. They would be after him. But he was thinking like the kid she'd once known, full of himself and his latest fantasy about how life was okay.

'Chrissy?' he said.

'Mmm.'

'There's something you have to know.' He lifted her face. 'The doctor says I can't have normal sex for at least three weeks,' he told her solemnly.

'Neil!'

He tried to grin.

'But he didn't say anything about abnormal sex.'

28

THE STREET WAS a sedate curve of tenements and two-storey houses. The small gardens at the front were neat and colourful and the view from the windows would be good. Tall trees and a park beyond.

It was a nice place to grow up in.

Number ten was halfway along, a main door flat, the front windows hung with flower boxes in full bloom. Rhona walked by on the other side, then walked back again, on the same side. When she reached the blue door she stopped and looked at the name above the doorbell, her heart racing. She just wanted to know. If they were there she would go away, she told herself, go away and wait for him to contact her.

The name wasn't Hope.

The woman who answered her ring was in her early fifties, with springy grey hair and glasses. She seemed unperturbed at finding a stranger on her doorstep and quite anxious to help. Rhona suspected she liked dealing in information of any kind, giving and receiving it.

'Sorry, dear,' she was saying. 'They left here four years ago and moved to England.'

'Do you happen to know where in England?'

There had been no forwarding address.

'Sorry I can't be much help, dear. Except, I do remember it was a big place they went to, with a university. Mr Hope was a lecturer in Geology, I think. He got a new job down there. Manchester, or Birmingham perhaps?' She shook her head. 'Rather them than me. They say Glasgow's violent, but we know better, don't we?'

Rhona walked back to her car. It was no good being disappointed, she told herself, she shouldn't have come anyway.

She climbed in and switched on the radio. As she turned the ignition, she decided she would go back to work. Try and forget all about it. Concentrate. Decide what she was going to do about Sean.

As she turned into the main thoroughfare she spotted the local primary school, its gates wide open. A sign was up on the railings giving details of the Polling Station hours. The playground was thronged with adults instead of children. Rhona suddenly remembered this was polling day. She slowed down and stopped, knowing he would be there.

He was on the steps, hand held out, a smile on his face. Edward Stewart, distinguished lawyer and happy family man, doing his bit to revive Tory fortunes in Scotland and looking, Rhona thought, every bit the next MP for this area.

She started up the engine and drove away. She had kept her side of the bargain. Let him have his seat in Parliament, she thought. With any luck it would mean he would be out of Glasgow most of the time and she would never have to see him.

The traffic was busy on the road back into town and Rhona cursed herself for having brought the car at all. It was hard enough to keep her mind on the traffic with all this fighting for her attention. Rhona was rewarded with an angry horn blast. She turned off onto the next side street and looked for somewhere she could get a coffee. In half an hour, the traffic would have dwindled and she might get back in one piece. She stopped at the first café and bought a large cappuccino.

Preoccupation wasn't the only problem. She had had little to no sleep the previous night. At three o'clock in the morning, she'd finally given up tossing and turning and switched on the light. If she was going to be tortured by thoughts of Liam, she might just as well have them with the light on. So she let herself think. And the more she thought, the more she wanted to see her son. She had lost years of his life, she didn't want to lose any more. Around four o'clock in the morning, she made up her mind. She would go to the address on the printout, check if the Hopes were still living there. She had never imagined they wouldn't be.

Rhona looked up, startled out of her thoughts by the waitress, who was asking if she wanted a refill. She nodded.

'You were miles away,' the waitress said.

'I was thinking about my son,' Rhona let herself say.

'Giving you bother, is he?'

'No. Not really.'

'Lucky you. I could see our Michael far enough.

Still. You only get a loan of them, don't you? That's what my mum says.'

Rhona nodded. It's the sort of thing her own mum would have said. She suddenly and achingly wished her mother was alive. Both of them still alive. Wished she had told them. Wished. Wished.

For months after her father died, she had imagined driving home, where he would be waiting for her as always. He would hug her and tell her how glad he was to see her. Silly. But it helped. Kept her going.

She was twelve years old when her dad told her she was adopted.

They had been at the cinema. It was a cold Saturday afternoon and they had had a chippy on the way home, for a treat. Her gloves smelt of vinegar because she had eaten half the chips with them on, until her dad said not to.

The news didn't bother her at the time. She wasn't even sure what 'adopted' meant, not until she was thirteen and her friend Louise told her all about sex and how babies were made. Even then, she didn't want to know who her real parents were. It didn't seem to matter.

Her mum had finally volunteered the information one day, while they were chopping vegetables together at the kitchen table.

'Your real mum was my cousin Lily,' she explained. 'She was a traveller, went lots of places . . . Italy, Egypt, Lebanon.'

It sounded romantic.

'She brought back this nice boyfriend once. He wanted to marry her, but she said no.'

'Why?'

It was the only question Rhona ever asked about her real parents.

'Our Lily was always her own woman. "Give a man a bit of paper and he'll think he's bought you." That's what she used to say.'

She stroked the chopped carrot into the soup pot.

'Your dad's name was Robert,' she continued. 'Robert Curtis. He was tall, blond and very handsome.' She looked fondly at Rhona's curly fair hair.

'They went off to Venice together and he fell ill with food poisoning. There were complications, and he died. It was a terrible tragedy. Lily came home to have you.'

She looked at Rhona.

'She was young. She didn't think she would be able to look after you properly. She asked us to take care of you.'

It seemed to Rhona that her life was being stirred round and round, like the soup.

'So, you came to us, and a lucky wean you've been too.' She touched the top of Rhona's head with a damp hand.

'Then Lily died in Istanbul and they buried her there. I wanted to try and bring her home but your dad said, no, Lily never thought of Glasgow as home anyway.'

That night, her mum had pulled out the big black tin

of family photos and showed Rhona her real mum and
dad.

Rhona looked out at the bright street busy with shop-
pers. Women with children, in prams and held by the
hand. She wondered again why she hadn't told her
parents about the baby. They would have been kind,
helped her look after Liam so that she could finish her
studies. It was just that her life had been so tied up with
Edward. And Edward didn't want to be a father. Not
then, anyway.

Rhona went to pay.

Her waitress was on the till.

'Don't you worry about him,' she told Rhona. 'If you
put the hours in, they turn out all right in the end.'

Rhona thanked her and left.

She realised she had unconsciously taken the route to
Police HQ when she found herself behind Garnethill.
She swore and hit the wheel, then resigned herself to
the prospect of a round trip back to the lab. She
ignored Garnethill's mesh of one way streets and
headed for Hanover Street. Suddenly she was on
George Square and hesitated long enough to miss
the right turn. God, she was literally going round in
circles. Then she spotted the magnificent pillars of the
Gallery of Modern Art. She could get to St Vincent
Street that way. She hit the brakes as a bus stopped
suddenly in front of her.

A teenager jumped off and stood hesitantly. A group
of goths were sprawled on the Gallery steps in the

sunshine, but this boy wasn't dressed like them. He was scanning the entrance, looking for someone, but whoever he was looking for wasn't there. His disappointment showed in the sudden droop of his shoulders.

It was then that she saw the man. He had been behind a pillar. He called out and the boy's face lit up.

The man didn't come any nearer. It didn't matter, because Rhona already knew who he was.

29

FIONA GAVE EDWARD a look that would have cut bread.

'Why didn't you keep him here?' she hissed. 'It doesn't look good for the photograph.'

'I couldn't help it.' Edward was at a loss. 'He just sneaked out without telling me.'

Edward could tell by his wife's face that it was not a good idea to pursue the matter. Amy's husband getting ill was damned inconvenient. The caterers had turned up, thank God, but Amy was the one to get the kids organised.

However, nothing was going to spoil this moment for him. Not even Jonathan's absence. He would only have put on one of those faces and ruined the photograph anyway. He would get round the problem by giving the press a family photo of their own to use, Edward told Fiona.

'Well,' he finished triumphantly, 'what do you think? Damn fine majority. Up a thousand on Labour's.'

'Sir James will be delighted.'

'Sir James *is* delighted,' he told her. 'He's been in touch. He'd love to be with us tonight, but he's flying to Paris in the morning. Sends his good wishes to you.'

Edward squeezed Fiona's arm affectionately. 'I'd better go and mingle,' he said.

The sitting room was full. Edward was well aware that he had not been everyone's favourite nominee and that there would be plenty to sort out once the celebrations had died down, but for the moment he accepted all the congratulations at face value. He walked about shaking hands, making a joke here, an interested enquiry there. Altogether, quite satisfying.

The French windows were wide open and people were spilling out into the warm evening. The warm sun made him feel even more contented. It had taken two long hard years to get here, but it had all been worth it.

He glanced over at Fiona. This kind of life was made for her. She was the perfect MP's wife. Discreet and supportive, and sexy enough to make him a source of envy among his fellow MPs. You only had to look at the other wives to see how lucky he was. Edward glanced around to confirm his view.

He wasn't too upset that she didn't want to be in London all the time. They had agreed against uprooting the children. Even so Edward couldn't imagine why Fiona would prefer to be in Glasgow during the week. But the arrangement could prove mutually convenient. He for one would be glad to get away from the daily round of family life, especially the constant friction with Jonathan. The thought of the bachelor life in London was most attractive.

Sir James had offered the use of his London flat for a few weeks until he found his own. Damn nice of him really, thought Edward. All mod cons plus housekeeper and no teenagers in sight, sound or smell. Perfect.

Edward's mind came back to the present. He looked over at the drinks table. Morag was there again, guzzling. Why wasn't Fiona keeping an eye on the girl, he asked himself.

He threw Morag a pointed look, but she either ignored it, or didn't see it. Edward was on his way over to tell her off when the boyfriend appeared by her side. He said something to her and Morag gazed up at him in adoration. Edward was impressed. Nothing he said to Morag elicited anything like such a response. And he had thought the guy was a waste of space.

It was nearly one o'clock when the guests started to leave. He and Fiona stood at the door and shook hands with everyone. Edward could see that Fiona was tired. But she wanted to end the evening properly. Show their supporters that she was made of the right stuff. At last, the house was empty.

'Will you lock up?' Her voice was tired.

'Morag?'

'Went to bed earlier. Too much champagne.'

There was still no sign of Jonathan.

'I'll leave the big lock off. He's not usually so late.' Edward switched off the lights in the sitting room.

They climbed the stairs wearily. For once Edward didn't feel like celebrating his victory by making love. He hoped that being an MP wasn't going to reduce his sex drive.

*   *   *

Jonathan locked the front door and went into the sitting room. The luminous dial of the clock on the mantelpiece showed four-thirty. Outside, the lawn spotlights cut a strip across the grass and bathed the front of the house in just enough light for him to see the clutter of empty glasses and filled ashtrays.

Amy hadn't been here tonight. She would never have left a mess like this. Thinking about Amy made Jonathan want to cry. Amy always believed the best of him, even when she knew the truth.

Jonathan found a vodka bottle. He poured himself a shot and took it over to the couch. Lobby must have heard him come in because he appeared at the door and plumped himself across Jonathan's feet.

The warmth and comfort of the dog's body made the lump in Jonathan's throat grow so that he thought he would choke. Tears of shame slid down his face. He swallowed the vodka straight. It seared his swollen tongue and bit his bruised throat. He gagged, reliving Simon's relentless onslaught on his mouth.

He gathered a cushion in his arms and cradled it, curled sideways on the couch, while the dog whined and licked his face.

30

NEIL PRESSED THE buttons, then moved the mobile to his other hand, put his arm round Chrissy and pulled her close. The side of his face was still swollen and bruised. Chrissy touched the puffy skin with her lips and he squeezed her shoulders.

'Maybe he isn't there?' she said.

Neil shook his head as someone on the other end lifted the receiver.

'I want to speak to Jim Connelly.'

Chrissy heard the woman tell Neil her husband was still asleep.

'I have to speak to him. Tell him it's important.'

'What the hell d'you want?' rasped Connelly. 'If it's something about the paper, you should have rung the office.'

'I didn't want the office.'

Chrissy watched the nerve twitch on the side of Neil's cheek. He was concentrating and she knew standing upright for so long was giving him pain.

'Just shut up and listen,' he said.

Neil gave Connelly enough information to get his interest, then set up a meeting. Chrissy heard a grunt of agreement. Neil was right. The journalist was hooked.

After the call, Neil slumped, as if his strength had given out.

'You need to lie down,' she told him.

For once he didn't have a cocky reply.

When Edward swung his feet out of bed the next morning, the floor rose to meet him.

He steadied himself on the bedpost, cursed, and reached for his dressing gown. His head beat like a drum and his stomach was heaving as if he was on a Channel crossing. He stood and waited until the floor stopped tilting.

As he headed for the shower, he tried to work out how much drink he'd had. It hadn't seemed that much, but he'd been talking and he hadn't had a lot to eat.

He was paying for it now.

He turned the shower knob to power. The needles beat down, but it didn't help the pain in his head. He promised himself some strong coffee and two headache tablets. Then he would be fine.

As he went downstairs, Fiona called out for him to check Jonathan's room.

'I didn't hear him come in,' she said.

Edward groaned, and climbed back up the stairs.

Jonathan's door was tight shut. Edward hated Jonathan to lock his door.

What if there was a fire, he asked himself. He'd said the same thing a million times before. It hadn't made any difference.

If he'd been smoking in there, and there was no point

in him denying he did it, there was even more chance of a fire.

Edward knocked firmly. Nothing. He tried again, harder this time.

'Jonathan,' he called loudly. 'Answer me, Jonathan. I know you're in there.'

The ensuing silence was like a grater on Edward's nerves. This time there was strength behind his anger. He pushed at the door and it moved slightly, then stopped against the bolt the boy had put on.

'Stupid thing,' Edward spat.

It was amazing how much the presence of that little bolt infuriated Edward. A little bolt that split his son's life from his own. Shut him out. His resentment was making him feel nauseous. He didn't have time for this. Not this morning. The presence of the bolt insulted him deeply and he had a desire to throw himself against the door with all his might, and fuck his headache. But he resisted the impulse.

He would keep his temper, he told himself. The door was perfect, apart from that stupid bolt. If he tore it off the door, it would harm the wood.

Edward knocked again.

'For Christ's sake, Jonathan. All you have to do is moan, then I can tell your mother you're alive.'

Silence.

Edward tutted loudly, and let go of the handle. He was fed up with this. If the door was locked, Jonathan was in there. He headed down the stairs.

*   *   *

While Edward was at breakfast, half a dozen calls came through, including one from Ian Urquhart. Everyone was delighted, Ian said. It was as if the Party had won a General Election. Mind you, thought Edward, winning a Tory seat north of the border felt much like that.

After mutual congratulations were over, Ian asked tentatively if Edward was willing to do a couple of interviews. Ian was savvy enough to expect him to be nursing a hangover.

Of course he was willing, Edward told him tartly, but it depended who it was to be with.

'Jim Connelly of the *News*?'

Edward made a face. He would have to feel a whole lot better before he was up to a meeting with Connelly.

Fiona finally appeared at midday. Edward was dealing with correspondence at the kitchen table.

'You don't look so good. Hangover?' Fiona suggested sweetly.

He looked up from his papers. 'I look a damn sight better than she does,' he retorted.

Morag was slumped over a plate of cornflakes, looking nothing like the livewire of the previous night. She didn't even acknowledge the comment.

'I have an interview here at two o'clock,' said Edward testily. 'I hope she'll be tidied away by then.'

'I'll make sure she's organised,' Fiona promised him. 'No sign of Jonathan yet?'

'No.'

Edward went back to work and Fiona gave an exasperated sigh.

'I think I'll go for my shower now,' she said.

He thought she was going to leave him in peace, but it was not to be.

'Do go and get him up and make him take a shower. Tell him to put on something half decent. You don't want the press to think you've got an imbecile for a son. Do you?'

Edward watched his wife disappear upstairs. If they had an imbecile for a son, he thought, surely it was Fiona's fault? He'd read somewhere that a boy got his brains, or lack of them, from his mother.

He climbed the stairs again, determined to get Jonathan's door open this time, even if he had to take it off the hinges.

The music was faint, but now that his head had calmed down, Edward was certain he could hear it. Jonathan must have his earphones in, and be completely oblivious to his shouts.

'Jonathan! I'm coming in now, Jonathan.'

Edward lowered his shoulder and gave a good sharp push. The bolt sprung off and hit the floor and the door swung open. The room stank of stale cigarette smoke. When he'd halved Jonathan's allowance, he'd hoped to put an end to that particular habit.

Edward walked briskly over to the window and drew the curtains. Sunlight swamped the room. That didn't do much for his fragile head. He reached for the catch, throwing it open with a resounding 'there', and turned towards the bed, ready to do battle. It was just as he'd thought. The little idiot had fallen asleep with the earphones in and the compact disc set to play over and over again.

Edward reached for the sleeping form, pulled out the earplugs and threw back the covers. Jonathan didn't move.

He was lying on one side, still wearing last night's clothes, knees pulled up against his chest, hands held protectively between them. His son's foetal position stopped the angry words in Edward's throat. Jonathan was fifteen years old, but lying like that he looked about five.

Edward touched the shoulder gently, then with more strength. Fear chilled his guts. An arm, suddenly released, fell onto the bed. Now Jonathan's head was turned towards him. Edward stared uncomprehendingly at his son's face. The lips were transparent, pulled back across the teeth in a grimace, the blue eyelids shut; and under Edward's terrified touch, the boy's skin was cold and slippery as a slug.

Edward rolled him over and shook him harder, consumed with panic.

'Jonathan! Wake up, Jonathan!'

He let the head fall back and stumbled to the door, the word 'ambulance' forming somewhere in his throat.

Fiona had come running from the bedroom. Behind her Morag stood, her hand over her mouth. It didn't silence her piercing scream.

When Edward opened his front door four hours later, Amy came hurrying out of the kitchen to meet him, ashen-faced. It was strange, thought Edward dully, how he had never thought about Amy before, not properly, not about her place in their lives.

When she asked how Jonathan was, Edward was suddenly sorry that he hadn't let her know. She had stayed here worrying all the time.

'He's still weak,' he said. 'They pumped his stomach but they're monitoring him for liver damage. The paracetamol does that, you know,' he explained in a voice resembling the one the young doctor had used to him.

'Dearie me, dearie me. The poor lamb.'

Amy was beside herself. He had always thought of Amy as the cleaner. Someone to give the kids their tea when Fiona and he were late back. Someone to child-mind when they were going out.

She was crying, the paper hanky soggy and disintegrating in her hands.

'There, there,' he said stupidly.

Amy had been with the family since Jonathan was born. Fiona had employed the odd nanny here and there; when she went to her bridge parties, her tennis club, the health club, but it had never worked. The kids just went down to the kitchen, to Amy. Amy had looked after them, always been pleased to see them. She, Edward realised with a start, had been their mother.

'Come on, Amy.' He laid his hand awkwardly on her shoulder. 'Why don't you make us both a cup of tea?'

She stood up, glad to do something.

'Yes, yes of course, Mr Stewart. I expect you're hungry. I've kept a nice bit of beef for you.'

Edward followed her to the kitchen. He suddenly didn't want to be in the sitting room alone.

'You sit down, Mr Stewart. I'll get your tea.'

Edward nodded and sat in the chair next to the stove while Amy bustled about, checking the side oven for the meat, pulling the big kettle over the hot plate. Lobby came and licked his hand. Edward suddenly wanted to cry. It was an unfamiliar feeling.

Amy set him a place at the table and ushered him over. While he ate, he told her that Fiona was staying at the hospital and that Morag had gone off with her boyfriend for something to eat.

'Oh, I should have said. Mr Urquhart phoned.' Amy looked apologetic.

'You didn't . . .'

Amy shook her head.

Edward nodded gratefully. 'I'll ring him as soon as I've decided what we say about this.'

'And a Mr Connelly from the *News*.'

Edward pulled himself together. 'Right. I'll get back to him after I've eaten.'

The food made him feel better. Edward pushed the plate and cup aside. 'I'd better go and sort things out,' he said.

Amy lifted the plate and nodded.

The sitting room was pristine again, the way Edward liked it. Amy had picked some roses and it was permeated with their light perfume.

It made Edward long for it to be yesterday again. Yesterday, when life was sweet. He replayed the previous evening in his head, but this time Jonathan was with him, chatting to people, being pleasant, helpful.

He saw himself putting an affectionate arm about his son's shoulders.

In the hospital corridor, waiting for them to finish emptying Jonathan's stomach, Edward had felt furious. What was the boy thinking about?

Suicide.

The doctor had questioned him closely. This young man, questioning him. What had Jonathan taken? Had he been drinking? Did he take drugs? How long ago had it happened? Was he depressed about something?

Stupid questions. Questions that had nothing to do with their lives. My son is a stranger, Edward suddenly thought, an aggressive, irritating, messy stranger, who simply inhabits an upstairs room in my house. If he was a lodger I would have thrown him out.

It was Fiona who told the doctor about the empty vodka bottle and the paracetamol packet. Fiona who said he had been depressed about his schoolwork, but had brightened up recently.

The calm before the storm.

What about his friends, the doctor asked.

What friends, Morag had said. Jonathan only ever talks to his computer.

Edward poured himself a whisky and paced up and down the room. Attempted suicide was an ugly phrase. He could not permit such a phrase to be used. He would have to tell Urquhart, but it must go no further than that. His heart contracted at the thought of Sir James finding out.

If all this had happened before the by-election! The thought was horrifying.

Anger began to replace regret. Anger at people who provoked incidents that screwed up his plans. Jonathan had no idea what he was doing.

But everything was going to be all right. It would be all right.

Edward climbed the stairs to Jonathan's bedroom. The window was open and Amy had cleaned up. The bed had been stripped and remade and the empty bottles removed. The stale smell that had irritated him earlier had gone. Edward began to move about, touching things, opening drawers, trying to find out what his son had been thinking about, however bizarre it might turn out to be.

The computer had been left on. He could hear the buzz. But the monitor was off. Edward decided he would take a closer look at his son's most prized possession.

His only friend, Morag had said.

The screen lit up, revealing a mass of icons. Edward tried double clicking on a few. One opened to reveal a set of revision notes for physics and Edward was momentarily pleased, until he noticed a line of expletives half way down.

Fucking school. Fucking physics. Fucking Cambridge.

It was baby talk. Baby talk with swear words. Typical!

He tried another icon. The desire to investigate his son's life was fading. He turned away. He needed to phone Urquhart. Organise those interviews. Get his head in order.

But something compelled him to turn back.

Two email messages were listed on the screen. One from Mark, who Edward remembered vaguely as a school friend of Jonathan's. The other was from someone called Simon.

Edward read them both.

31

BILL'S GUT FEELING had never let him down before and he was sure it wasn't letting him down now. The call from Connelly had convinced him of that.

Sir James's fast exit to Paris was too damned convenient. The Super had informed him that he could speak to Sir James's lawyer during his absence. Sir James was more than anxious to help.

Oh yes, thought Bill. About as willing as a Protestant is to genuflect.

Janice was waiting for the next move.

'Right. It's time to organise a search warrant.'

Janice was goggle-eyed. 'Where for, Sir?'

'Sir James's country house. Falblair, I believe it's called.'

'Sir?'

'Or more precisely, Janice, the cottage at Falblair.'

Jim Connelly was not used to daylight, Chrissy thought. He looked like a man who thought trees and green grass belonged on the telly.

He was walking towards them along the gravel path. Chrissy knew it was him, although she had never seen him before. He looked like a man who needed a drink, she thought. She'd seen that look before. Too often.

Neil couldn't stand upright for long and he was leaning on the bridge railing, as if he was interested in the sluggish brown water below.

She nudged him gently.

'He's coming,' she said.

The pub was halfway along the road to Charing Cross. Neil nodded at the barman. He and Chrissy went to a booth near the back, leaving Connelly to get the drinks. The barman poured two vodkas without being asked. Connelly ordered a ginger beer with ice.

Neil took a mouthful of the vodka and licked his bruised lip carefully.

'Someone tried to spoil your looks,' Connelly said.

'Aye.'

'Want to tell me why?'

'I had some photos. They wanted them back.'

'The bloke you were talking about?'

'His friends.'

'So what do you want me to do?'

Neil was studying the reporter closely.

'I think there's five of the bastards.'

His hand was gripping Chrissy's now, the nails digging into the flesh. She had to stop herself from crying out.

'I've only seen one of them, but he talks about the others. They all use different names. One's called Simon. He's the one that works the computer stuff. The one I know calls himself Caligula. He thinks I don't understand why, but he's wrong.'

Neil looked over at the door. Someone had come in. The barman returned his gaze and shook his head.

Connelly was toying with his drink, waiting for Neil to go on.

'Caligula likes it rough,' Neil said. 'He's into tying something round my neck, tightening it till he comes.'

'That's the way Jamie Fenton died,' Connelly prompted.

'I know.' Neil nodded at the barman and two more vodkas appeared. Connelly dug deep in his pocket and pulled out a tenner. Neil waited until the barman had gone before he went on.

'The last time it happened I split when it got too rough. The stupid arse hadn't tied me tight enough. Too fucking excited.' He took a slug of vodka. 'We go to a cottage in the garden of a big house. He takes me there and brings me back. I don't get to see where we're going. He ties something round my eyes and my hands. Likes his fun in the car,' he explained matter-of-factly.

'Do you know where this cottage is?'

'No.' Neil stretched the torn lips over perfect teeth in a bizarre semblance of his old smile. 'But I saw someone leave the place once. A car stopped at the gate. There was a man and a woman inside. I saw their picture in the paper this week. He's called Edward Stewart.'

'Christ!' Connelly nearly choked on his ginger beer. He slammed the glass down. 'I know where that is. It's Falblair. Country estate of Sir James Dalrymple, Edward Stewart's lord and master.'

'So?'

'So. He could blow us both away.'

Neil stood up, dragging his hand from Chrissy's. Expletives erupted from between clenched teeth. Chrissy took hold of his arm.

'Don't, Neil.'

'When I saw that bit in the paper I thought you'd be different, but you're not. You're just like the rest of them.'

'Sit down and shut up.' Connelly's anger matched Neil's. 'I have to think, don't I? I have to think, how we do this properly. I take it you want to get them?'

Neil stared at him, then sat down. 'Fucking too right I do.'

'Good. So do I.' Connelly smiled. 'And I want to wipe that smug look off Edward Stewart's face and stuff it right up his arse.'

32

EDWARD RESCHEDULED HIS interview with Connelly for half past four. Then he rang the hospital. Fiona sounded calmer.

'Jonathan's much better,' she told him. 'But there's still a chance of liver damage. If only you had found him sooner.'

Edward ignored the note of blame and told her he would come back to the hospital after his interview.

'What have you told Ian?'

'I've told him the truth. He thinks he can keep it low key.'

'It would be better for us all if he did.' She wished him luck.

He would need all the luck he could get.

He had wondered whether to tell her about the email, but something stopped him. He didn't want anyone to know what he had read on that screen.

Not even Fiona.

After he'd read the email, Edward had gone to the bathroom to be sick. After that, he stormed about the house, swearing at the top of his voice.

When he calmed down a little, he began to reason with himself.

What would happen to Jonathan if he told the police the whole story? Edward shuddered. It would be terrible. They would question Jonathan about this . . . this homosexual relationship. It was probably all nonsense anyway. Kids said things they didn't mean on email. Showing off.

No. He had to keep things quiet, for Jonathan's sake. He must wait until Jonathan was out of danger and they got a chance to talk. His responsibility was to protect his son.

Jonathan would need peace to get well. He could not cope with a barrage of questions right now. God help us, Edward thought, if the press gets wind of this.

He didn't want to hear the small voice that spoke of other children caught in the paedophile net. Children who might be saved, if he told the police what he knew.

His own child must come first. Whatever happened, he must not panic. He would inform the police, but not yet. He would sort it all out once Jonathan was better. For his sake, the family must not be dragged into a scandal.

Edward was regaining his composure. He would concentrate on this interview with Connelly. He had weathered storms before this, he could do it again.

But Sir James would have to be told, he realised. He had supported Edward, put his name forward. He would have to tell him.

Edward left a message with Sir James's secretary in Paris, asking him to return the call as soon as he was able.

Then he sat down and began to prepare for his interview.

Rhona heard Tony answer the phone elsewhere in the lab. She was halfway to the door to ask who it was when he appeared.

'Chrissy says she's sorry. She's not very well. She'll be in tomorrow.'

'Right.'

'She also said, tell Rhona not to worry.'

'Thanks.'

Tony stood for a moment as if he expected her to say more. When she didn't, he shrugged and went back to work.

At least she knew Chrissy was okay. From the guarded message, it sounded as if nothing too bad had happened to Neil, either. But the call only dealt with one of her worries. She had still to decide what to do about Gavin without the input of Chrissy's common sense.

Gavin could have seen her awkwardness on Monday night as the result of the computer search and realised the child she was looking for had something to do with her personal life. He was no fool. But was he evil?

Evil. The description seemed ludicrous. She felt comfortable with Gavin, instinctively trusted him. She should have asked for an explanation straight out. Why was she doubting him? She'd jumped to conclusions. Just as she'd done with Sean, she thought. Sean had known that, no matter what he said about the woman in the Kelvingrove Gallery, he had already been tried and convicted.

Rhona tried to keep her mind on her work, but it was no good. By five she was eaten up with a mixture of frustration and fear. She had to do something.

When Bill came on the line, Rhona stuttered out a story about a man she met at a party called Gavin MacLean who'd said he knew Bill, and she wondered . . .

'Is this you checking out your dates with me now?'

She tried to sound light.

'Who else can I check with?'

'So what do you want to know?'

'He said he worked with the police.'

'And?'

'Is it true?'

There was a moment's silence.

'It is. Though he shouldn't have mentioned it. Must have been trying to impress you.'

She tried to laugh.

'Gavin MacLean runs a company called Cyber Angels. He specialises in forensic computing. He analyses what's on hard disks, tracks computer fraud, identifies hackers, that sort of thing. He's working with us on the paedophile case.'

'Right. Thanks.' As relief swamped her, Bill came back on.

'Is this you changing the man in your life?'

'Well . . .'

'Pity. I liked Sean. Good on the sax, too.'

Mercifully he didn't wait for a reply.

In the light of what Bill had said, both the email and the sighting of Gavin at the Gallery of Modern Art could be seen as innocent. If Gavin was helping the police blow a paedophile ring, he would intercept correspondence relating to that. It was obvious. And as for the Gallery. Why shouldn't he meet a young man at GOMA? she asked herself. He had two nephews, he'd told her so.

At that point, Tony stuck his head round the lab door and made her jump.

'Just wondered if it was okay to go now.'

'Of course. I'll clear away and lock up.'

Rhona heard the main door of the lab bang behind him and then there was silence. She cleared her table and packed everything away. If Gavin phoned tonight she would explain that she didn't want to see him at the moment. She had to sort things out with Sean before she got involved with anyone else.

On the way home she stopped at the library and went through *Which University?* in the reference section, noting down the names and phone numbers of every big university with a Geology Department.

What was she going to do with the list? Work her way through, asking every one if there was a Mr Hope on the staff?

She laid down her pen, knowing she couldn't do it this way. If she found Mr Hope, he would guess why she had contacted him. If she was an adoptive parent and a woman phoned out of the blue, looking for her son, what would she feel? She would be terrified that someone was going to take her son away from her.

Hopelessness washed over her. It was no use. It was all too late. Much too late.

The librarian was walking towards her. Rhona forced herself to look up and acknowledge the fact that it was closing time. She slipped the piece of paper in her pocket and left.

33

BILL KNEW HE was taking a chance on this one and he didn't need reminding.

'You're sure, Sir?'

'Get on with it, Janice.'

'The Super won't like it.'

'I'll deal with the Super, Constable.'

'Right, Sir.'

Janice gave him an odd look. It wasn't because he was making things difficult for her, he knew that. She was worried for him.

'Just tell them to find something.'

'I'll tell them, Sir.'

He had spent most of the day in his office, dealing with paperwork he'd been avoiding since the beginning of the investigation. When the call came through from Dr MacLeod he had been momentarily nonplussed. It was not Rhona's style, neither the question nor the manner in which it had been put. It started him thinking.

He certainly wouldn't be happy if Gavin MacLean had been talking to anyone about the work he was doing for them. There had been enough of a furore after Connelly's coverage. That had almost brought the investigation to a complete halt.

Damn. He was sorry if Rhona had finished with the Irish chap. Folk today just didn't stick it out, he thought. Not like Margaret and him. Twenty-four years. And, God knows, Margaret had enough reason to leave him, considering the life of a policeman's wife.

This investigation had got to Rhona. It had got to him. Crawled into his guts and twisted them about.

He buzzed Janice, glad he hadn't sent her to Falblair.

'Janice.'

'Yes.' Her voice was as cautious as his own.

'What do you know about Gavin MacLean?'

She looked surprised. 'He was checked out before we employed him, Sir. As far as we know he's clean.'

'I don't mean that. I mean, socially.'

'Socially?'

If Janice wasn't trying to be obtuse, she was a natural.

'Is he married?' he tried again.

'No.'

'Do you fancy him?'

'Sir!'

'Well?'

'No.' She was emphatic.

'Why not?'

There was a pause. 'Can't say, Sir.'

'Go on, Constable.'

'He's too good to be true, Sir.'

'Thank you, Janice. That's a great help.'

If she noticed the sarcasm, it didn't show in her face.

'Is that all, Sir?'

*   *   *

The call came through at 4.40. The cottage at Falblair had been searched thoroughly.

It was Sergeant George. 'Sorry, Sir. No curtains.'

Bill swore under his breath. He was in for it now. Connelly's contact must have been lying.

'But,' the voice on the other end stopped him, 'we did find something that might be useful.'

As Bill listened a smile spread over his face. His Sergeant was right. This was as good as the curtain, maybe even better.

'Drop it in at Forensic on your way back,' he said. 'Make a point of giving it to Dr MacLeod in person.'

There was someone at the door. She didn't want to see anyone right now. Rhona sank back down into the bath water and closed her eyes. She had promised herself a long hot soak, and then . . . she had rehearsed the words a hundred times. She was going to tell Sean everything. Why she hadn't answered his calls, why she hadn't gone with him. Her suspicions about him. About herself.

The bell went again, more urgently this time. The sitting room light was on. Whoever it was knew she was in, and wasn't giving up. She swore, got out of the bath, put on her dressing gown and headed for the intercom.

'Chrissy! Come up.'

Neil was with her.

Rhona led them into the kitchen.

'Vodka?'

He nodded.

'Straight?'

'Any way.'

Chrissy accepted one too. She looked as if she hadn't slept for a week.

'You'd better tell me everything,' Rhona said.

'Is this journalist going to help you?' Rhona said when Neil finished.

'He said he would contact the police. Give them the information.'

Chrissy was slowly regaining her colour. She looked at Neil, who was standing by the window. 'It's just that when we got back to the flat, there was this car. A car Neil recognised.'

'You can't go back to the flat, not yet anyway. You must stay here.' Rhona wasn't prepared to take no for an answer.

Chrissy looked at Neil, willing him to agree.

Neil gave in – 'Just for tonight.'

Rhona had made up her mind. 'There's something I want to show you.'

She came back with the printout.

'You used the names Simon and Caligula.'

He stared at her. 'Aye?'

'I think you should read this.'

She watched as his eyes swept the page.

'What is it?' Chrissy looked worried.

He looked at Rhona. 'Where did you get this?'

'From the printer on Gavin's computer.'

'Who the fuck's Gavin?'

'The computer guy I told you about,' Chrissy said. 'He was looking for information for me,' Rhona explained. 'Hacking the system, if I'm honest. He works for the police, helping them track computer crime.'

Neil examined the printout closely. Then he asked why the string of letters and numbers at the top of the page were the same.

'What?' she asked stupidly.

'The two email addresses are the same,' he said. 'Look.'

Rhona grabbed the paper from his outstretched hand. He was right. Her brain was straining to recall anything she could about the subject, but she kept coming back to the same conclusion.

'Neil.' The thought wouldn't go away. 'Have you ever met Simon?'

Neil's face tensed.

'Slimy shit! There isn't a Simon and a Caligula. There's just one creepy bastard. And I've seen that bastard's face.'

Rhona came back with the vodka bottle.

'Do you think it was Caligula or Simon that murdered the boy?' she asked Neil.

'I don't know,' he said.

'We'll have to tell the police,' Rhona said.

'No.' Neil was adamant. 'Wait. This MacLean. If he's working for the police then you would expect him to have information like this. Why didn't you ask him? Why did you hide the printout? Chrissy thought you and him were getting it on.'

Rhona interrupted, shaking her head. 'Chrissy was right. I did like him. I *do* like him.'

She was finding it hard to explain. 'I felt guilty, like I was spying on him, his work. Then I saw him with a boy.'

'What d'you mean, with a boy?'

A boy got off a bus near GOMA. He met a man. It looked like Gavin.'

'Did you know the boy?'

'No. But Gavin's got two nephews. It could have been one of them.'

'What does he look like, this Gavin MacLean?' Neil cut in.

'He's tall . . .'

Chrissy interrupted her. 'He's blond and wears a tweed jacket. Good looking. Smiles too much.'

Neil shook his head.

'You don't think it's Gavin?' Rhona asked Neil.

'No.'

He stood up.

'You two stay here,' he said.

'Where are you going?' asked Rhona.

Neil bent down and planted a kiss on Chrissy's mouth.

'Don't let anyone in. I'll see you later.'

The place seemed suddenly empty without him. Rhona followed Chrissy over to the window, as sorry as she was to see Neil go.

34

CHRISSY PERSUADED RHONA to go and finish having her bath, while she cooked them both something to eat. Afterwards they took the remains of the vodka through to the sitting room and turned on the television.

It was the news.

'Sure you want to watch this?' Chrissy said.

Rhona nodded. There was always a chance they might have caught the guy, and life could get back to normal.

But no. A spokesman for Strathclyde Police made a statement that there were no further developments to report, but new lines of enquiry were being pursued.

'They're bound to catch him now,' Chrissy said angrily. Rhona felt unable to say what she was really thinking. Whoever Caligula was, he was a clever operator. It looked as if he had been at this game for a long time and, if what Neil said was true, he had friends in high places. If Neil chose to testify against any of them, they'd hire top lawyers to tear his story apart.

After the murder update, the news switched to political stories, leading with the Conservative victory. Rhona listened dispassionately as the commentator spoke of the dynamic campaign fought by the blue-eyed boy. A photograph of a happy family of four appeared on the screen. It had been taken in the garden of a big house. Fiona, Rhona had to admit, looked ravishing. At the front stood a plump but pretty teenage girl and a slightly younger boy.

The boy looked as if he would prefer to be anywhere rather than in front of that camera. Rhona felt a surge of pity. She knew how Edward could persuade people to do things they didn't want to do.

The voice-over gave an inventory of Edward's distinguished legal career, his climb through the Party and his successful bid for power. Edward made a statement saying that his victory showed he had the heart and will of the people and he would do his utmost to put forward the Scottish perspective in parliament. He intended taking a flat in London, returning to Glasgow at weekends to see his family and conduct constituency business.

'Had enough?' Chrissy's voice broke in.

'Yes.'

As Chrissy reached for the remote, the family picture was replaced by a more recent snapshot of the boy, sitting in a bedroom with a black labrador between his knees. The report continued with the news that Edward Stewart's son Jonathan had been admitted to hospital soon after the by-election for an unspecified reason. He was expected to make a full recovery.

'Why don't we put some music on?' Chrissy suggested. Rhona didn't answer. She knew where she had seen Edward's son before.

*   *   *

'You'd better phone Edward.'

'And say what?' Rhona looked at Chrissy. 'Say I saw his son meeting a man I thought I knew at the Gallery of Modern Art? He'll tell me I'm being hysterical.'

'What about the boy's name in the email. You said those low-lifes talked about a Jonathan.'

'There are lots of Jonathans. It could even have been a code name.'

'Rhona. You know and I know it's probably a coincidence, but if you think for a minute there was anything strange about that meeting, you've got to phone Edward. If he knows Gavin, we can at least relax about this one.'

'I know.'

The phone rang out unanswered. Wherever Edward was, he wasn't at home. She was expecting an ansaphone to click on when a breathless voice came on.

'Hello. Yes? This is the Stewart residence.'

'I'm sorry to bother you. I'm trying to get in touch with Edward Stewart.'

'They're all at the hospital. They've been there all day.'

'I saw something on the news about Jonathan. I hope he's going to be all right?'

'He's off the danger list, but it was touch and go for a while.' The woman was gabbling on in her distress. 'What could have possessed the poor lamb to do such a thing?' she mumbled, as much to herself as to Rhona. 'He takes things too much to heart.'

Rhona gave her condolences and rang off.

'Well?' said Chrissy.

'Edward's at the hospital,' Rhona said. 'The house-keeper told me Jonathan was off the danger list, but it was touch and go for a while.'

Chrissy looked puzzled. 'If you saw him on Thursday, it must have been something pretty sudden.'

'That's the funny thing,' said Rhona.

'What?'

'The woman said "what could have possessed the poor lamb to do such a thing?"'

'What thing?'

Rhona didn't like what sprang to mind.

'You don't think Jonathan tried to kill himself?' she said.

'Why would he do a thing like that?'

'It's just that the woman said he took things too much to heart.'

'My mum used to say that to me,' said Chrissy grimly. 'How else are you supposed to be?'

35

JONATHAN WAS DREAMING.

The dream was nice and he didn't want to wake up. He was back in his bedroom. Amy had cleaned it, so he had nothing to worry about any more. He heard Lobby barking and went over to the window. Lobby hardly ever barked. His mother was always saying he wasn't much of a guard dog any more. Too old. To Jonathan's surprise and delight, he saw the labrador running across the grass like a puppy. It made Jonathan feel like a kid again, like when he used to hide up the apple tree, or go swimming in the river. Before he got embarrassed about everything.

The dog had disappeared into the woods.

Jonathan waited for him to bound back out. He could hear barking but Lobby didn't reappear. The dog was with someone. Someone who had called him, and now wouldn't let him come back. Jonathan was frightened.

'Lobby. Here, boy. Lobby,' he called.

Then there was someone saying his own name, someone in the room with him.

He turned towards the voice. He knew that voice. He didn't like that voice.

'It's me, Jonathan. I've come for you.'

*   *   *

'It's okay.' Someone was lifting his hand in theirs.

Jonathan opened his eyes.

A nurse smiled down at him. 'Was it a nightmare?'

He shook his head, embarrassed, but Nurse Jenkins didn't seem to notice. 'I'll just check your temperature, then I'll leave you in peace. Your father will be in shortly.' She gave an encouraging smile. 'Right. Do you want your earphones over?'

She handed him the portable CD player from the bedside table and four CDs.

'I like this one,' she said. 'I'll borrow it when Sister goes off duty.' She gave him a conspiratorial look and smoothed his covers. 'I'll be back later to check you're okay.'

Jonathan wished he could speak to her. He liked Nurse Jenkins (her first name was Rachel, he'd heard one of the other nurses call her that). He worried at first that she might despise him for what he'd done, but she didn't. She told him the first time she met him that she understood. Once it had happened, that was the turning point, she said, things got better after that.

But did they?

Jonathan put in his earphones and turned the sound up. If the music was loud enough, it would shut out the nightmare.

36

BILL PUT THE phone down, then picked it up again. If
there was the smallest suspicion that Connelly's in-
former was right, then he had to speak to Rhona.

It rang half a dozen times, then a sleepy voice
answered.

'Chrissy?'

'Yes!'

'It's Bill Wilson. Thought I'd got the wrong
number.'

'I'm staying with Rhona for a couple of days. I'll go
and get her.'

Bill heard the pad of feet and Chrissy's voice. A few
seconds later, she was back.

'I don't understand. She was here when I went off to
sleep.'

'When was that?'

'About ten. We were watching telly together. She
said she was tired and went to bed. I conked out on the
couch.'

'Was there any reason for Rhona to go out?'

Chrissy didn't seem too keen on answering that
one.

'Chrissy, this could be important.'

'I don't know. Maybe she just went out for a walk. She was upset earlier.'

'Why was Rhona upset?'

'I don't know.'

Bill knew he was wasting his time. If Chrissy and Rhona had secrets, Chrissy wasn't going to give them away.

'When Rhona gets back, will you ask her to get in touch with me?'

Chrissy agreed.

Bill Wilson wasn't happy. Ever since that call from Connelly, he'd had an uneasy feeling he was missing something.

Rhona didn't like leaving without any explanation. But she wasn't even sure what she planned to do.

She drove around the quiet streets for half an hour, wondering why she was out there, wishing she could talk to Sean, hear his calm voice unravel this mess that had become her life.

At ten o'clock she'd told Chrissy she was going to bed. It seemed pointless waiting for Neil to come back, since they had no idea when that might be. She had drifted off to sleep for a couple of hours till the nightmare woke her up. She lay in bed, shaking. If she didn't do something, she would go mad.

So here she was, driving around in the middle of the night, planning to tell her ex-lover his son might be in danger from a paedophile ring. She was making a total fool of herself.

Rhona pulled in and switched off the engine. She

reached into her bag for her mobile. It obeyed her spoken command and showed Edward's number. She pressed okay.

Edward answered. If it had been Fiona's voice she would have put the phone down.

'Rhona! What the hell are you doing? It's one o'clock in the morning.'

'I had to ring you.'

'Rhona. If you're still on about . . .'

'Shut up, Edward. It's about Jonathan.'

'Jonathan?'

He was taken aback.

'I think he's in trouble. Has Jonathan ever mentioned someone called Simon?'

'What?' Now Edward was giving her his full attention.

'Answer me, Edward. Does Jonathan know someone called Simon?'

Rhona drove straight to the hospital. If Edward left home right away, he would get there ten minutes after her. With the engine turned off, silence settled heavily round her. It was funny. Here she was, seventeen years later, waiting for Edward to come and meet her at the same hospital. Only it was the middle of the night. And this time, it wasn't her child.

On the evening she had been admitted, Edward took her to Accident and Emergency and handed her over to a nurse, then cleared off. Rhona had tried to make a joke of it. Her boyfriend, she told anyone who would listen, was allergic to hospitals. Allergic to babies would have been nearer the mark.

The silence was split by the sound of a siren. It sent a shiver down Rhona's back. She watched as the ambulance drew up, and the latest emergency was rolled in through the front doors. At least in her job she wasn't expected to save lives.

Edward heard out her garbled story about paedophiles using the Internet to locate vulnerable kids. She'd told him about the email she'd found and the man she saw with his son. For once, Edward didn't interrupt. Instead, he had asked her to meet him at the hospital. He had something to tell her face to face.

Rhona felt dog tired. She would tell Edward everything she knew, then it was up to him. She would be able to forget about it and go home. She'd tell Sean she was coming to Paris.

A figure she thought was Edward was approaching. He tapped on the car window and she leaned over and flipped the passenger lock. He slipped into the seat beside her.

'Hello, Rhona.'

'Gavin!'

'I couldn't believe it when I spotted your car,' he said. 'What on earth are you doing here?'

Rhona couldn't find her voice.

'A friend was involved in an accident,' she managed. 'They've decided to keep her in overnight for observation.'

Gavin was looking at her strangely.

'Why are you here?' Rhona asked.

'My nephew has suspected appendicitis and since I'm in charge this week, while my sister and her husband have a week's holiday . . .' Gavin paused. 'Are you sure your friend's all right? You look very worried.'

'She's fine. I'm going to head home now.'

Gavin opened the door. 'Okay. I'd better get back and find out what's happening.' He paused, meeting her eyes. 'Can I give you a call tomorrow?'

Rhona nodded.

'Good.' He smiled back at her.

Rhona watched him walk back to A&E. Only then did she admit to herself how scared she was.

It took ten more minutes for Edward to appear and during that time Rhona swung wildly between suspecting Gavin and feeling like a complete idiot for doing so.

'What man?'

Edward was looking at her as if she was insane.

'The man I told you about. The one that works for the police.'

'He's here? Why?'

'He said his nephew has been admitted with appendicitis.'

'And you don't believe him.'

'I'm not sure . . .'

'This is the guy you saw Jonathan with?'

She nodded.

'The guy with the printout?'

'Yes.'

'Right. Let's go and find out if he's telling the truth.'

The A&E entrance was lined with trolleys as if there had been an earlier catastrophe that had filled the hospital. Inside, the reception area was as Rhona remembered, apart from a lick of paint and a Trust Hospital sign on the wall. The nurse in charge wore her name above her left breast on a similar label, but she looked just as tired and overworked as the one that had admitted Rhona all those years ago.

Edward explained that he was there to look in on his son, and pushed his card across the desk. The nurse gave it a quick glance, recognised the name and said that would be fine. Mr Stewart could go up quietly, please.

He gave one of his charming smiles and the nurse's face lit up. He asked her if they had recently admitted a boy with suspected appendicitis.

'I think it might be the nephew of a friend of mine.' The nurse nodded.

Yes, there was a boy with appendicitis on the ward now. 'He's been sedated,' she said. 'They're planning to remove the appendix in the morning.'

'Thank you.'

Edward looked at Rhona. Wrong again, his expression said. Before they went upstairs, he delivered a few pleasantries about the dedication of the NHS. The nurse was completely charmed.

37

SOMEONE HAD BRUSHED Jonathan's hair back from his face. For the first time Rhona could see it clearly. He looked like his father, she thought, but his delicate nose was Fiona's.

The charge nurse smiled at them as they passed, obviously recognising at least one of the late-night visitors.

There was an enormous bunch of flowers on the table at the window and the trolley beside the bed held a personal stereo and a pile of CDs.

'We shouldn't wake him,' Rhona said, her heart aching at the thought of standing in that room, looking at Edward's son. A son they didn't share.

'He won't wake. They've sedated him,' Edward said, the strain coming through in his voice. He led her into a side room with a coffee machine, a television and a phone.

'What luxury,' said Rhona.

'I need to work while I'm here,' Edward explained. 'The hospital is very understanding '

He waved her to a seat.

'The papers don't know . . .' Edward began, finally. 'Jonathan apparently tried to kill himself.'

He looked at Rhona's concerned face. 'I'm sure it's all a mistake,' he insisted. 'Jonathan had been drinking. Vodka. And we found an empty bottle of paracetamol.'

Rhona said nothing.

'I believe he overdosed by mistake.'

It didn't sound like the truth to Rhona. 'Where does this Simon come into this?' she asked quietly.

Edward crossed to the door and closed it.

'There was an email on Jonathan's computer from someone called Simon,' he said. 'It made me think Jonathan was in trouble.'

'Oh, Edward.' Rhona stood up and went towards him, suddenly overwhelmingly sorry for this man she had hated for so long. 'What did the police say?'

'I haven't told them,' he said firmly.

'You have to. If Jonathan is in danger, you have to tell the police.' Rhona was remembering another young face on a dirty pillow.

Edward threw her an agonised look. 'I can't, Rhona. It would ruin everything.'

'Does Fiona know about this email?'

He shook his head. 'You're the only one who knows.'

'You can't do this to me, Edward!' She was furious. All he cared about was his reputation. She was even more furious at herself. If only she had told Bill Wilson what she suspected, instead of phoning Edward.

'You can't blame me for protecting my son.' His voice was moving from defensiveness to defiance.

'You're not protecting Jonathan,' she said scornfully. 'You're protecting your own career.'

There was a moment's silence. Then Edward said, 'You once made that choice yourself. Remember?'

Jonathan knew his father was in the room. He didn't want to open his eyes. He didn't want to see him or speak to him.

He wanted to drop back into oblivion, but his father's voice was getting in the way. And there was another voice, a woman's voice. It wasn't his mother and it wasn't Nurse Jenkins. It sounded angry. Even in the state he was in, Jonathan was pleased that someone was angry at his father.

One thing was certain, they wouldn't be discussing what he had done. He knew that officially this had never happened. He was in hospital for a minor operation, that was all. Edward Stewart's son would never have tried to croak himself. That would be too embarrassing. The nurses had been warned to say nothing to him, he was sure of it. Only Nurse Jenkins showed that she knew. He hadn't had a visit from the psychiatrist. Even his mother didn't go beyond standard bedside chat, you'll be home soon and not to worry. Amy was the only one he wanted to see, and she wasn't allowed to visit.

'You'll see Amy when you get home,' his father had said, as though Amy was a household pet.

The room was in semi-darkness, with the small light above his bed angled away from his eyes. He thought about listening to another CD. He settled the earplugs in place and lay back down and closed his eyes against the world.

* * *

If he had not put the earplugs back in, he would have heard the door open. As it was, he heard nothing until the hand was over his mouth.

A voice was whispering in his ear.

'There's nothing to be frightened of. It's me, Simon. I've come to get you out of here.'

He turned towards the voice.

'You do want out of here, don't you?'

If he agreed, Simon wouldn't hurt him.

'I'm going to take my hand away now. Then we can talk. Okay?'

Jonathan nodded.

'There. Sorry about that.' Simon stood up.

'Where did they put your clothes?'

'I can't go away with you,' Jonathan blurted out. 'My parents will be angry.'

'You're nearly sixteen. An adult. You can leave home when you like.' He smiled. 'We'll leave them a note.'

'I don't want to.'

Simon's eyes clouded over.

'I haven't any money.' Jonathan was clutching at straws.

'Oh,' said Simon, his face growing pleasant again. 'That's not a problem.'

He threw some clothes at Jonathan.

'Who was that in the room with you earlier?'

'You mean my father?'

'No, the woman?'

Simon's eyes were cruel. How could he have liked those eyes?

'I didn't see her.'

Simon was at the door now, looking down the corridor.

'Right. I know you like playing games. Let's play.'

He produced a roll of twine and a knife.

'Turn round.'

Terrified and ashamed, Jonathan did as he was told.

'And let's make it even better . . .'

Simon forced the gag into his mouth.

Outside the air was cool. Simon had resumed his caring voice, telling Jonathan not to worry, there was a blanket in the back of the car in case he got cold. Jonathan stumbled down the metal steps of the fire escape, praying that Nurse Jenkins would look in on his room now and raise the alarm. But the window above him stayed dark. His room was three storeys up. Twice Simon stopped him, thrusting him down on the cold metal steps, until he was sure there was no movement behind the fire doors on each landing. On the first floor landing, he held the knife close to Jonathan's face and in the faint light of the emergency bulb, Jonathan recognised it. How had Simon got hold of it? It couldn't be the same one. If it was, Simon had been in his kitchen. Jonathan felt sick.

At the bottom of the fire escape steps, Simon made him sit down while he checked the car park was clear. Jonathan frantically scanned the darkened windows above him, willing someone to look out.

'Right. Come on.'

He was bundled round the side of the building

towards the shadow of a car. The gag was tight and it was hard to get his breath. They were at the car now. Simon forced Jonathan low, looked round, opened the back door and pushed him in.

Jonathan collapsed onto the seat.

'There,' said Simon triumphantly as he climbed in and locked all the doors. 'And just to prove how much I've been thinking about you . . .' He lifted something white from the front passenger seat, buried his face in it, then threw it over the back. 'Recognise this?'

Jonathan's stomach turned over. This time the smell was his. Simon had his tee-shirt, and the only place he could have got it from was his own room.

'How do you like our new game?' Simon smiled down at him for a moment before the blanket covered his eyes.

When Rhona got home, the hall light was on and there was a message on the pad from Chrissy. DI Wilson wanted to speak to her. It was four in the morning. Surely Bill wouldn't want to hear from her at this hour? She glanced in the sitting room. Chrissy was asleep on the couch. So Neil hadn't come back yet.

She would call Bill first thing, she decided. She set the alarm for seven and rolled gratefully into bed.

38

BILL HAD SLEPT through thirty-six murders in his time as a policeman. That made an average of three a year for the past twelve years.

During all those investigations, he had never once discussed his thoughts with his wife. He didn't want her to feel disgust at what was rattling round his head.

For the last four days he had been waiting for the next death. That thought lay behind every move he made. He was willing to put his job on the line to prevent it.

Searching Sir James Dalrymple's cottage on the say of a male prostitute had done just that. He argued to the Super that everything was justified by finding the curtain tie-back that matched the one round the dead boy's neck. The Super did not agree. There are thousands of tie-backs like that one, he had growled. And although they had gone over the cottage with a fine tooth comb, that was all they had got.

Connelly was adamant about his story. The rent boy had had sex there with a guy who called himself Caligula. He reckoned Caligula and Simon were one and the same man. Why didn't Bill see what Rhona

MacLeod had to say about it. Which he'd tried, but her mobile was switched off.

What he had to go on amounted to next to nothing, and he knew it.

'Come back when your rent boy agrees to give us a proper statement,' the Super said dismissively. 'Then we'll talk to Sir James.'

Back in his own office, the first call he took was from a Rachel Jenkins. Jonathan Stewart was missing. He had left a note in his room, but she was sure he would never have left it of his own accord. Bill asked if she had informed the family. She sounded contemptuous as she described how unwilling Edward Stewart had been to inform the police.

A woman after my own heart, decided Bill.

'Don't move anything, and don't let anyone in till I get there.'

When Bill arrived at the hospital Edward Stewart was waiting. It took him a full hour to begin to get the truth.

'After you told Dr MacLeod about Jonathan, where did she go?'

'She said she was going home.'

Bill pulled out his mobile and stabbed in Rhona's home number. Chrissy answered. The station had sent a police car to pick up Rhona, she said.

When Bill finally got through to Janice, she confirmed that no one at the station had contacted Rhona MacLeod that morning.

'And there's no answer from Gavin MacLean. The

beat Constable went round first thing. A neighbour said he'd gone to look after his nephews while his sister is on holiday.'

'When Gavin calls in, I need to speak to him.'

Edward was suddenly all ears.

'Gavin MacLean. He was the man Rhona said she'd met in the car park. He said he was with his nephew. Reception seemed to confirm that. Rhona had found something at his flat that suggested he might be involved with Jonathan.'

'Go on.'

'An email from someone called Caligula that mentioned a Jonathan. She reckoned that MacLean working for you explained it.'

Bill listened grimly. He left Stewart and dispatched a Constable to check at reception. If MacLean's story was genuine, the hospital would have his sister's address.

The Constable was soon back with the news that there had been an appendix case the previous night and the mother was at her son's bedside.

'His mother?'

'Yes, Sir. She came with him in the ambulance. A tall, fair-haired man was seen near the waiting room. No one saw him after that.'

'And the mother. What did she have to say?'

'Never heard of any Gavin MacLean.'

'Contact the station. I need a search warrant for Gavin MacLean's house and I want the Stewarts' house searched thoroughly too.'

'Have we got Mr Stewart's permission to do that, Sir?'

'We will have, Constable. Count on it.'

39

RHONA WAS GOING to be sick. It was like a nightmare fairground ride. She bounced between the metal walls of the boot, bashing against one, then the other, willing the contents of her stomach to stay where they belonged.

She was losing the battle when the car began to slow, throwing her abruptly against the boot lid; then it accelerated again, but not as fast now. It felt as if they had been travelling for about an hour. They could be anywhere within a sixty-mile radius of Glasgow. She braced herself for the next turn.

Rhona had barely been asleep an hour when the phone had woken her. Chrissy got there first.

'Neil?'

Chrissy shook her head.

'They want you down at the station right away. They've sent an unmarked car. It'll be waiting at the end of the street,' Chrissy told her.

'Right.'

Rhona got dressed, stuffed more money into her pocket and headed for the door.

'Don't worry,' she called. 'Neil will be back soon.'

Chrissy nodded, unconvinced.

The cloudless morning sky promised a warm day. Rhona walked briskly towards the corner. She would tell them everything. She would support Neil's story. Jonathan would be safe. And to hell with Edward.

She hurried over to the waiting car. As the driver got out she called 'Good morning', thinking it would be someone she knew.

It was.

Gavin MacLean was still smiling when Rhona felt the car jack hit her head.

When she first opened her eyes in the suffocating darkness, Rhona thought she had been buried alive, and adrenalin filled her body. Her hands were tied behind her back and in a blind panic she kicked wildly at the metal walls.

So often she had arrived at a murder scene, to find a body trussed up just as she was now. She had taken blood samples, urine, semen. She had swabbed the victim's fear and carried it back with her to the laboratory. For her it was a puzzle to be solved. This time it would be Tony carrying the swabs back to the lab. Tony who would ask Chrissy to carry out the tests.

No! She would not think like that. If Gavin had wanted to kill her, he could have done it many times before now. He was going to dump her somewhere, give himself time to get away. She just had to be calm, think straight. And she must not be sick. She could not be sick with this gag in her mouth. She had to find a way to take her mind off the nausea.

Then she remembered. When she was pregnant and suffering from morning sickness, she would take her mind off it by humming a tune.

Rhona began to hum through the gag. She managed the first few notes, then the next few. She got to the end and began again. The third time through, she realised what it was. It was the tune Sean was playing when she first saw him.

She would not die. Chrissy would come looking for her, Chrissy and Neil and the police. Bill Wilson would find her. She was going to stay alive and she was going to keep Jonathan alive.

Rhona realised she hadn't heard the boy now for several minutes. At first she had heard him crying, the heartrending sound seeping down through the back seat and into the boot. She had tried to call to him, to let him know she was there, but the gag completely muffled the sound.

The past five minutes they had been travelling on a rough track. The car had been bumping up and down, throwing Rhona heavily against the roof and floor. Now they were slowing down. She braced herself as the vehicle drew to a halt. It seemed an age till the boot opened and she could smell water.

She was so dazzled after being in the dark that she couldn't focus as she was dragged from the boot, her legs buckling under her.

'Come on, Dr MacLeod. Come and see your holiday cottage.'

Gavin prodded her along a path and into a low white cottage. After the bright daylight, her eyes now had to adjust to the dim hallway. She felt the stairs before she saw them and tripped forwards, knocking her shin. Irritated by her clumsiness, Gavin pushed in front of her and began to haul her up behind him. Then, as they turned on a landing, she was in full light again. He stopped at the first door and thrust her inside.

He propelled her towards the far wall and shoved her hard against it. Her head slammed off the plaster. The explosion of pain disorientated her. He suddenly released his hold and her legs gave way. She found herself sinking to her knees in front of him, her face level with his crotch. He wrenched off the gag and looked down at her, blocking her efforts to draw back. She realised with horror that she was trapped between him and the wall.

He grabbed her hair and yanked her against him. She gagged as her face met the bulge of his erection.

'It's all your fault, Rhona. I was only going to the hospital to remind our young friend to keep his mouth shut.'

He jerked her face upwards.

'Then I met you. You don't hide as much as you'd like to think. I asked myself, why would sweet little Rhona be frightened of me? And I remembered the other time you looked at me like that. The night I found your son on that list.'

'I wasn't frightened.'

He looked down at her pityingly. 'You're a bad liar, Rhona. I always know when you're lying. All that crap about Sean, when you really wanted me to fuck you. Well, you're about to get your wish. But let's not hurry

246 *Lin Anderson*

things. It was fun watching you. And finding children is my speciality.'

His words had a sickening impact on Rhona.

Liam. Had she led him to Liam? And all those other vulnerable young people. Children that Gavin only knew about because of her.

'What have you done with Jonathan?'

'He's downstairs. I mustn't be too long. He's waiting for me.'

She had to keep him away from Jonathan.

'Leave us tied up. We won't be able to get away. We won't tell anyone about this.'

He shook his head.

'I have plans for Jonathan.'

'If you stay, they'll find you. Neil knows who you are. Neil will tell them where to come.'

Gavin gave an ugly laugh.

'Didn't you know? The rent boy's dead.'

'No.'

'He didn't know when to shut up.'

He reached for his zip, his breath coming in short sharp gasps.

'You killed Jamie Fenton.'

Gavin ran his tongue over his lips. 'We don't kill during sex. Not on purpose. Certain . . . routines . . . can heighten sexual pleasure. The boy knew the risks. We pay them enough.'

'Enough to die?'

'People die all the time.' He pulled his cock free of his trousers. 'They come looking for it. Jonathan came looking for it. I only gave him what he wanted.'

She had to keep him talking.

'He's only a child.'

'Poor misunderstood little Jonathan. His parents didn't want him.' He gave her a hard look. 'But you would know all about that, Rhona. You gave your own child away.'

He was playing with himself, getting pleasure from her fear.

'Caligula thinks we should kill you both. But that's rather extreme.'

'Don't talk as if he's another person, Gavin. I know it's you.'

He sighed.

'Caligula is me and I am Caligula.'

He placed his hands round her neck. The pressure drove her mouth open.

'Who else knows that, Rhona?'

She was almost blacking out from lack of oxygen. Her muscles were going into spasm. With a flood of shame she felt hot liquid run down her legs, pooling on the floor.

'Who else knows about me?'

The sudden drill of his mobile shattered his concentration.

He released her throat and she keeled over.

Gavin glanced down at Rhona, his face expressionless. Without a word he left the room and went downstairs. Rhona pulled herself up. There was some slack in the cord. With a huge effort, she could free her right hand from its bonds. In his preoccupation with the call, Gavin had left the door open. This was her chance.

She stood on the landing, gripping the stair post, listening.

Jonathan lay spreadeagled, hands and feet secured to the corners of the bed. Simon was outside talking on his mobile. Jonathan twisted his body in a desperate last effort to get free.

Gavin had finished his conversation and was coming back inside. He started up the stairs. Rhona froze. Suddenly, he stopped as if something had occurred to him, and went back down.

'I was going to keep you all to myself. We were going to have a little weekend up here on our own. Good food, good wine and all the time in the world for games.'

Simon's smile made Jonathan's skin crawl.

'And now you've spoiled it.'

'Don't look at me. I don't want you to look at me.'

Simon sighed.

'I don't want to look at you. And neither will any of the girls, once they find out what you've been up to.'

'Shut up!'

'Shut up?' Simon's face was a mask of distaste. 'I don't think so. I say what goes. I'll say whatever I like . . . and do whatever I like.'

'Don't you fucking touch me.'

'Caligula was right. You're not my type, after all.'

40

THE GLASS DOOR opened and Janice came out of the cubicle. Bill looked up hopefully. She shook her head.

'He's still unconscious, Sir.'

Bill looked through the glass panel at Chrissy's worried back.

'The doctor says he's lucky to be alive.

'How did Connelly find him?'

'Neil phoned, said he was meeting someone in the park near the bandstand. Someone Connelly should see. When Connelly got there, Neil tried to tell him something before he passed out. Something about a loch. They're at the loch, he said.'

'They're at the loch?'

'Yes, Sir.'

'We're not short of lochs round here,' Bill snapped. 'The Trossachs, Loch Long, Loch Lomond. Spoiled for choice. Have you asked Chrissy what she thinks?'

Janice shook her head.

As Bill pushed the door open Chrissy looked up at him defensively. She wasn't going to let him try and question Neil, that was for sure.

Bill pulled a chair up beside her. She was holding Neil's hand.

'His mother wasn't in,' she said quietly. 'It was his father that answered the phone. I told him Neil was in hospital.' She paused. 'He said he didn't have a son called Neil.'

Chrissy fell silent.

'There's something you might be able to help me with. Connelly heard Neil say the word loch before he passed out. Do you know what he meant?'

She looked at him puzzled, and then realisation suddenly dawned.

'Yes,' she said triumphantly. 'I think I know where he meant.'

41

JONATHAN FELT SWEAT prickle the side of his face.

Simon had stopped talking to him.

Now he was muttering quietly to himself.

Jonathan lay very still.

Simon looked at him as if he had suddenly remembered he was there.

He went over and opened a bag, lying in the corner. Jonathan saw the leather straps and a whimper escaped his lips.

'This is what you came for. This is what you like, isn't it, Jonathan?'

Simon was coming towards him, saying his name over and over again.

Jonathan's long cry propelled Rhona downwards, even though she didn't know what she would do when she reached the bottom. The cry abruptly ended in an ominous silence. Rhona stopped dead. It seemed an age until she heard another sound. Relief flooded over her. Jonathan's weeping meant he was still alive.

She could hear him moaning, a pitiful searing sound. Rhona couldn't bear it. She had to get Gavin away from Jonathan, even if it meant bringing his attention back to her. Her eyes darted round the hall. The front door still stood ajar. There was a chance that, if she hid behind it, she would be out of his line of sight.

She shut the front door and opened it again, then slipped behind. She heard footsteps. If Gavin went upstairs, she was sunk.

She stopped breathing as he lurched past her and went outside.

Rhona immediately threw her whole weight behind the door and slammed it shut. She slid the bolt home.

Jonathan looked up at her, his eyes half-crazed with fear.

'Who are you?'

'A friend.'

Rhona tugged at the cord that tied his feet to the metal bed. Her bruised hands fumbled, her fingers swollen and clumsy. Then she caught sight of the kitchen knife on the floor beside the bed. The end of the blade was too thick to slip between the boy's ankle and the cord. She would have to slice in the other direction.

'Stay as still as you can.'

She began sawing. The cord's disintegration was achingly slow, but at last Jonathan could wrestle his feet free. The leather strap binding his hands was easier. He sat up and wrenched off the tasselled cord from his neck, revealing a brutal welt.

'Did he take your mobile?' Rhona asked urgently.

'It was in my pocket.'

He pointed at a jacket behind the door. Rhona

started frenziedly going through the pockets. She was on the last one when she heard a window smash. Jonathan threw her a look of panic.

She thrust the mobile towards him.

'If you can get a signal, call 999. They'll trace us.'

He nodded. 'Where are you going?'

'To make sure he doesn't get back inside.'

Rhona picked up the knife and slipped it under her belt. She grabbed the poker from the fireplace, and opened the door.

Smoke was drifting through the hall. It seemed to be coming from a door at the back. The bastard was trying to burn them out, she thought. Without thinking, she ran over and flung it open. The smell of petrol hit her. Fire was already licking its way along the floor beneath the broken window. She might be able to smother it with the curtains. She made a move forward, then realised she was too late and dashed back into the hall. Behind her, the room burst into flames.

They were a mile outside Arrochar when the radio buzzed in the police car. The driver answered it. A fisherman, taking full advantage of the long Scottish day, had seen smoke coming from a holiday cottage on the far side of the loch and used his mobile to call the fire brigade.

'The brigade are on their way, Sir.'

DI Wilson ordered the driver to turn on the siren and get a move on.

* * *

The hands that circled Rhona's neck came from no-where.

'You never give up, do you?' Gavin's voice was a demonic hiss.

Rhona dropped the poker and grabbed at his fingers, trying to prise them apart. He leaned back, lifting her bodily from the floor. Her neck was ready to snap.

She scrabbled in mid air, grabbing at nothing. Then her right hand touched metal. The knife. She pulled it free and swung it sharply over her left shoulder.

Everything happened in slow motion.

The point met Gavin's eye. She felt the momentary resistance as it pierced the membrane. Then it was through. He staggered backwards. She heard a scream, but whether it was his or her own, she had no idea.

Free of his grip, she slumped against the wall, gasping in the smoke. Jonathan was shouting at her, urging her towards the open door.

'I'm coming!'

She staggered towards a vision of loch and sky and air filled with sweet oxygen.

Bill was out and running even before the car came to a complete halt. The cottage was engulfed in flames. He ran towards the fire engine, scanning the group of figures for her fair hair. Then he saw her.

'Rhona! Thank God.'

She was holding a boy's hand.

'This is Jonathan,' she said. 'He wants to go home.'

Bill said a silent thank you to whoever was listening up there.

'The hospital for both of you, first.'
Rhona looked grey.
'Gavin's still in there.'
Bill looked at the inferno. He was glad.
'He fooled me.' Anguish filled her face.
'He fooled us all,' said Bill gently.

42

'YOU WANTED TO see me, Sir.'

The Super didn't look up but went on reading the buff-coloured report on his desk. Bill waited.

When he did look up, his face was furious.

'I thought I told you to stop harassing Sir James Dalrymple.'

'There are certain aspects to this case . . .'

The Super's expression halted Bill in mid flow.

'I understand Fenton's killer confessed to Dr MacLeod and that he is now dead.'

'No, Sir.'

'What?'

Bill took a certain pleasure in the effect the news was having on his superior officer.

'We can't be sure Gavin MacLean died in that fire.'

'Does Dr MacLeod know this?'

Bill shook his head. 'The news is just in, Sir.'

'But you've pulled in five men suspected of being involved in this paedophile ring?'

'Suspected, yes.'

'Sir James had nothing to do with this.'

'I have reason to believe . . .'

'You have nothing to go on, Detective Inspector.'

'But . . .'

'Nothing but your bizarre obsession with implicating him.'

'He did rent out his hunting lodge to paedophiles.'

'We only have a rent boy's word on that.'

'Neil MacGregor saved Dr MacLeod's life.' Bill's voice was thick with anger.

'And for that we're grateful.' The Super became more conciliatory. 'The rent boy . . .'

'He has a name, Sir.'

'The rent boy admits that he was always blindfolded when he was taken to this place, doesn't he?'

It was clear where all this was heading.

'The lodge was thoroughly searched. Forensic found nothing at all to support his story. Is that not the case, Wilson?'

Bill held his silence.

'Sir James was out of the country when all this happened. I repeat, Detective Inspector, he has nothing to do with this case. I suggest you concentrate your efforts on finding Gavin MacLean.'

With a curt nod, he indicated that the interview was at an end.

43

'SIT DOWN! YOU were told to rest and put your feet up.'

'I'm not an invalid.'

Chrissy gave her one of her looks.

'Okay, okay,' Rhona relented. 'But you'll have to turn the telly on for me.'

Chrissy dropped the remote in Rhona's lap. 'I'm off to the hospital.'

'I hope you don't boss Neil like this or he'll stay in there for ever.'

Chrissy wasn't listening.

'Oh, someone phoned while you were napping,' she said as she went to fetch her coat. 'He said he would phone back.'

'It wasn't Sean?'

'Not this time.'

'Probably Jonathan,' said Rhona.

Chrissy had her coat on. 'I'll see you later,' she said.

'Tell Neil I was asking for him,' Rhona called after her.

The phone rang fifteen minutes later.

Rhona was watching the news. They were interviewing Edward. The new Conservative MP was being congratulated on helping the police track down five suspected members of a paedophile ring that had been operating in the Glasgow area. It had been a particularly difficult time for Mr Stewart, the interviewer explained, because the MP's own son had been kidnapped from his hospital bed by one of the men involved and had been in danger of losing his life. Rhona pressed the off switch just as Edward gave a special vote of thanks to Sir James Dalrymple for his support at this trying time.

'Is that Dr Rhona MacLeod?'

'It is.'

'I'm sorry to bother you.' The voice paused nervously. 'My name's Liam. Liam Hope.'

'Liam?'

'And I think I might be . . . your son,' he said.

'Oh yes, Liam,' Rhona said. 'Oh yes. You're absolutely right. You are.'

Bill watched Rhona take in the news about Gavin. Sitting in the armchair in her dressing gown, she looked pale and vulnerable.

'He's still alive.'

She said the words as though she already knew.

'I wondered.' She looked up at him. 'When he grabbed me in the hall. He came in by the back door. He must have got out that way.'

'We're running a check on all the hospitals. If he did escape, he'll need medical attention. We'll pick him up soon.'

She looked haunted.

'We've got mountain rescue teams checking the surrounding hills, just in case he's hiding out somewhere.'

She pulled her dressing gown tighter round her.

'I wish Sean was here with you.'

'Don't worry about me. I've decided to go to see Sean in Paris.'

'You're flying?'

Rhona shook her head. 'You know me. I like my feet firmly on the ground. A sleeper and a trip through the tunnel.'

44

THE TRAIN WAS slowing down.

Rhona didn't search for him on the crowded platform. He would be there, she knew that. Taking her time, she lifted her small case from the rack.

The carriage door opened with a sigh. The smell of French coffee from the railway restaurant reminded her how she would watch him move about the kitchen; a glimpse of thigh, an arm reaching up, his penis swinging soft and vulnerable. And he was always whistling.

He was standing near the barrier, watching for her. He smiled and waved. His face was so familiar that the horrors of the recent past dissolved, and all she knew was the smell of him, the taste of him, the warmth of his body next to hers. How could she have let herself get so close to losing this man?

He came forward and took her case.

'How are you?' he said.

'I'm fine,' she said. And it was the truth.

He put down the case.

'There are things I have to tell you.'

She put a finger on his lips to stop him.

'Just hold me.'

He put his arms around her and she buried her face in his chest.

'We've both been stupid,' she said.

They kissed.

'You taste like Ireland,' he said.

As they walked to the Metro, he asked if she had seen her son and she said not yet, but she had spoken to him.

'He wants to come to university in Scotland.'

'So he's clever, like his mother.'

They left the station arm in arm. And as they walked, Sean began to whistle, a tune so sweet that the sound of it in the Parisian street caused people to turn and smile.